PRAIRIE ROSE

1912. Working as a schoolteacher on the Canadian prairie, Paula Scott is courted by Jake Marriott, the father of one of her pupils. Her friends consider him a good catch, but Paula is secretly in love with Charles Ingram. Charles, however, is engaged to selfish society beauty Lola King. Paula knows she must forget Charles, but would it be fair to wed Jake when he can only be second best in her heart?

Books by Catriona McCuaig
in the Linford Romance Library:

ICE MAIDEN
MAIL ORDER BRIDE
OUT OF THE SHADOWS
ROMANY ROSE
DOWN LILAC LANE
AT SEAGULL BAY
GHOST WRITER
WHEN THE DAFFODILS BLOOM AGAIN
DARK MOON
TO LOVE AGAIN
IN A WELSH VALLEY
BITTER HARVEST
CHERRY STONES
HEART OF DARKNESS
FOLLOW YOUR HEART
A FAMILY AFFAIR
VICTORIAN SUMMER
HEARTS IN EXILE

CATRIONA McCUAIG

PRAIRIE ROSE

Complete and Unabridged

LINFORD
Leicester

First published in Great Britain

First Linford Edition
published 2013

A catalogue record for this book is available from the British Library.

ISBN 978–1–4448–1794–2

Published by
F. A. Thorpe (Publishing)
Anstey, Leicestershire

Set by Words & Graphics Ltd.
Anstey, Leicestershire
Printed and bound in Great Britain by
T. J. International Ltd., Padstow, Cornwall

This book is printed on acid-free paper

A Girl Wronged

Paula Scott trudged home, longing for a cup of tea. Philip Rowse was one of her least favourite pupils and half an hour of listening to him thumping away on the piano was almost more than she could stand. The child didn't have the slightest interest in learning the instrument, so why his mother insisted on the lessons was a mystery.

Paula sighed. Who was she to complain? If it wasn't for proud mothers like Harriet Rowse nobody would want piano lessons, and Paula would be out of pocket. Of course, it would be wonderful if one of her pupils turned out to be a child genius, but such prodigies were hard to find in Wimbledon.

Paula's own mother, Lydia, had been one of those proud mothers. She had convinced her daughter that she was destined to become a concert pianist, performing on the great stages of the world. Paula had believed that dream until the day her hopes came crashing down.

'She is a competent enough pianist, Mrs Scott,' her elderly teacher had explained, to Lydia's dismay. 'She'll sail through her examinations, and after that I can see her performing in amateur events, but I'm afraid Paula just doesn't have that spark that leads to greatness.'

The old man had gathered up his music sheets, shaking his head ruefully. Crushed, Paula had eventually come to terms with her disappointment. Now grown-up, she went from house to house giving private tuition, hoping to pass on her love of music to others, but it was an uphill battle.

'I can't do it, Miss Scott,' Philip had wailed, flexing his chubby fingers. 'I'm going to ask Papa if I can do fencing instead. Don't you think that would be a good idea?'

'I'll see you next week, Philip. And do try harder. I'm sure you'll get better with practice.'

And that was a lie, if ever there was one. Paula didn't know when she'd met a more ham-fisted child!

Quickening her step she soon came in sight of home, a neat villa on a pleasant tree-lined road. Paula passed through the creaking gate and entered the house.

'Is that you, dear?' Lydia trilled.

'Yes, Mother,' Paula called. She took off her hat, shaking out her fair hair where it was flattened by the felt.

'You look tired, dear,' Lydia remarked as she came in. 'I hope you don't have to go out again this evening.'

'I think I'll go to bed early and read my library book. They had the new Annie Swan in at the library. Miss Cowley kept it for me under the counter.'

'I do like her novels. Perhaps I'll read it after you.'

The front door slammed, and Lydia called out.

'I do wish you wouldn't slam doors, Bertie! You know how it makes my poor head ache.'

'Sorry, Ma! Is there any hot water? I want a bath.' Her son dashed up the stairs without waiting for an answer.

Paula pulled a face.

'What's got into him? He doesn't dress for dinner.'

Lydia smiled indulgently.

'There's a young lady in the offing, I expect. And why not? Your brother is a most eligible young man.'

'That's a matter of opinion,' But Paula's remark was drowned out when Bertie came clattering down the stairs.

'There are no towels. How am I meant to dry myself?'

'Elsie must have forgotten to put clean ones out. I'll send her up in a minute.' His mother frowned. 'You're home early, aren't you? I hope you didn't come away without permission!'

Bertie shrugged.

'The job? I chucked that. No scope for originality, as I told old Braikie when I handed in my notice.'

'Oh, not again, Bertram Scott! How many jobs are you going to chuck, as you call it? At the rate you're going, nobody will take you on at all.'

'Don't fuss, Ma! It's not as if we're broke. Why don't you send me off on the Grand Tour of Europe? That would help me put in the time until I come into my inheritance. That would be so much better than messing about with ledgers all day in a dusty old office. Anyway, can't stop to chat, unless you want a flood. I left the bath water running.' He bounded up the stairs again, whistling.

Lydia sank down on a brocade-covered chair.

'Where did I go wrong with that boy, Paula? Can you tell me that? And what am I going to do now? I haven't the money to send him abroad, and well he knows it.'

'You could ship him off to the Colonies,' Paula said, trying to lighten the atmosphere.

'There's no need to be so unkind. Your brother is just a bit immature, that's all. And the same thing applies. I can't afford to pay his way in Australia or Rhodesia or somewhere like that. You children seem to think I'm made of money. The trouble is you don't seem to understand how much it costs to run a house like this.'

Paula had heard it all before.

'I'm sorry, Mother, but I simply must go and get out of these tight shoes. I'm sure I'm getting a blister on my heel.' She needed a wash before the gong went for dinner; that was if Bertie ever got out of the bathroom!

Lydia seemed to have recovered her equilibrium by the time they dined. She said nothing when Bertie grumbled about the consommé. She asked Paula about her day.

The doorbell rang insistently. Lydia looked up from her lamb cutlet in annoyance.

'Who can that be at this time? People should know better than to call in the evening, when civilized people are sitting down to eat.'

They could hear Elsie's timid question at the door, followed by a loud barrage of words in a male voice.

'Should I go, Ma?' Bertie half rose to his feet, throwing his linen napkin down on the table as he did so.

'No, dear, just wait and see. It's probably not for us at all. They have come to the wrong house.'

A flustered Elsie came into view, wide-eyed.

'If you please, mum, there's a man.'

'Yes, Elsie. Who is it? What does he want?'

'I'll tell you what I want, madam! I want to deal with the young scoundrel who has got my daughter into trouble, that's what I want!' A large, red-faced man in a tweed suit and a bowler hat loomed in the doorway.

Lydia looked him up and down with great dignity.

'I don't know who you think you are, my good man, bursting in here like this, and I should think you might take your hat off, too. There are ladies present!'

'Very la-di-dah, I'm sure! Well, you won't be so hoity-toity when you hear what I've come to say. Mildred! Get yourself in here and face the music!'

The girl who sidled into the dining-room was pretty in a rather common way, despite the defiant look on her face.

'Hello, Bertie!' she simpered.

'Hello, Mildred.'

Looking from one to the other, Paula was surprised to see that Bertie didn't seem ashamed, just slightly puzzled.

'Do you know these people, Bertie?' Lydia asked.

Bertie nodded.

'Then I think we must hear what they have come to say. Elsie will show you into the sitting-room,' she told the man, 'and we shall join you in a few moments. I wish to speak to my children first.'

* * *

Paula hovered in the doorway, ready to rush out if things took a turn for the worse. She had to admire her mother, who sat upright on a high-backed chair, looking every inch the lady of the house, in complete charge of the situation. Bertie was slumped in an armchair, not meeting anyone's eye, while his girlfriend — if indeed, that was what she was — crouched low on the sofa, staring down at the carpet.

Her father stood beside her, with one firm hand on her shoulder.

'Won't you sit down, Mr . . . ?' Lydia invited.

'The name's Price. Joshua Price, and no, I'll say what I've come to say standing up.'

'Very well, then. Perhaps you'd like to tell us what all this is about.'

'That son of yours,' Price snapped, jabbing a finger in Bertie's direction, 'has got my poor girl in the family way. And I'm here to see what he means to do about it.'

Lydia glared at her son.

'Is this true, Bertram?'

'Of course not, Mother! You know me better than that!'

'There you are, then,' Lydia told Price. 'I'm sorry for the difficulty Miss Price finds herself in, but obviously my son is not responsible. There is nothing we can do to assist you. My daughter will see you out. Paula?'

'Please come this way, Mr Price,' Paula told him, but the man was not about to give up so easily.

'I say that the young devil is responsible, and must pay for his fun. Come on, our Mildred! Speak up and tell these people what he's done!'

The girl raised her eyes slowly.

'It's like Dad says. You've got to marry me, Bertie. Please, please, you must!'

Bertie's look of scorn would have melted an iceberg.

'She's lying, Mother! I swear to you, I don't know a thing about this!'

Joshua Price took a threatening step forward.

'I know you've been seeing our Millie, for I've seen you calling for her at the house. It's clear to me what's been going on, and there's only one way to put matters right!'

'Yes, it's true that we've been out walking once or twice, but nothing more than that! If Millie says otherwise, she's lying. Well, you won't pin this on me, and that's flat!' Bertie leaped to his feet and stalked out of the room.

Millie Price began to sob.

Lydia stood up.

'I think it would be best if you took your daughter home, Mr Price. I hope that you find the man responsible, because it is certainly not my son. Good day to you.'

Pulling his daughter upright, Price headed for the door.

'You mark my words, Mrs Scott. You've not heard the last of this. I'll make that young scoundrel pay. I'll get him for breach of promise, if nothing else!'

When the pair had gone, Lydia

collapsed into a tapestry-covered wing chair, clutching her chest.

'Fetch my pills,' she gasped.

Paula raced for the medicine cabinet, aware that the doctor had diagnosed her mother's occasional palpitations as panic attacks. The pills were nothing more than a mild sedative, but they had been effective in the past.

When Lydia had swallowed two of the tablets and was sitting back, perspiring slightly, Paula had time to think about the scene they had just witnessed. It was like one of the plays she'd seen on occasional visits to the theatre. There had been the wronged maiden, the irate father and the villain of the piece.

Her brother had been cast in the latter role, but was it an accurate portrayal?

Bertie, summoned downstairs to explain himself, was adamant that he was innocent.

'But you do know the girl?'

'Of course I know her, Ma! We met at the tennis club and she seemed a jolly sort of girl. I took her out once or twice; nothing special, just for walks and to a tea shop.'

'Do you swear that you didn't interfere with her in any way, Bertram?'

'Of course I didn't! What do you take me for, Ma? I suppose I might have kissed her once or twice, but nothing more than that. Besides, all that was ages ago. She wasn't my type, and I dropped her. It's weeks since I've seen her.'

'Then why . . . ?'

'Isn't it obvious, Ma? She's managed to get herself in a fix, and she's decided to pin it on me. Naturally her old man wants her to get safely married, to give the babe a name, but for some reason her chap can't, or won't, do the decent thing by her. Perhaps he's married; who knows. But her father has forced her to name the chap and she's picked me. Well, it won't wash; Ma, and that's all there is to it!'

Lydia leaned forward to pat him on the hand.

'Well, dear, of course you mustn't even think of marrying the wicked girl! I'm just sorry that all this unpleasantness has happened.'

A thought occurred to Paula. She frowned.

'But why you? I can see why she might not have wanted to name the father of her child, but surely she knows other men besides you? From the tennis club, for instance.'

Bertie went red.

'I suppose I might have boasted a bit.'

'Boasted? What about?'

'About my inheritance,' he mumbled.

'I see. You explained that when you turn twenty-five you'll come into money and your whole life will change.'

'Well, where's the harm in that? It's all true, Paula.'

'Bertram Scott, you're a fool! You've set yourself up nicely, haven't you? The girl saw her chance, and took it!'

'But she knows I'm not the father of her baby, and she couldn't possibly expect me to marry her.'

'Ah, but has she convinced Price of that? What's that revolting modern expression? Mud sticks! You heard what the man said. They'll drag you through the courts if they can, and the Scott name will be sullied.'

'Ma, I've told you I've done nothing wrong! They can't force me to marry the stupid girl. Let them do their worst!' He marched out of the room, head held high.

Lydia began to rock back and forth in her chair.

'What are we going to do, Paula?' she wailed.

'Perhaps nothing will come of all this,' Paula said softly. 'Price will get the truth out of his daughter, and we'll never hear from them again.'

'Where money is concerned some people will stop at nothing. And what about us? If this story gets out we'll be finished in society. You can say goodbye to your precious music pupils, too. No decent mother will want her children taught by a girl tainted by scandal.'

'Then what can we do?'

Lydia brightened suddenly.

'We'll send for Cousin Charles! What's the good of having a solicitor in the family if one can't call on him in time of need? He'll know what to do. Perhaps he can write an official letter or something, threatening the Prices with court action if they don't stop all this. I'll draft a telegram and you can post it first thing in the morning.'

Childhood Love

Charles Ingram was a tall man, without an ounce of excess weight on his body. With his black hair and intense blue gaze he reminded Paula of one of the old Stuart kings as seen in history book portraits. She had been half in love with him since a shy five-year-old and Charles a solemn boy of ten. She had followed him around like a little puppy, but he had always been kind.

Although he was known as Cousin Charles he was not actually related to the Scotts. Lydia's cousin, Mabel, a stout, rather plain woman, had long ago accepted the fact that she would probably never marry when she had met Max Ingram, a widower with a small son. Somehow they had hit it off and to everyone's surprise they had married after knowing each other for just five weeks. At forty-eight there was no hope of Mabel producing babies of her own, and she'd poured out all her love onto young Charlie, who had thrived under the attention.

Lydia and Mabel had been school friends and close chums as girls, and they kept up the relationship until Mabel's death in 1906. It was good to have someone to rely on, as Lydia found out when her husband passed away and Cousin Max came forward to help with settling his affairs.

Now Charles was here, standing on the hearthrug in Lydia's home, while she peered up at him, her expression full of hope and trust. Paula sat beside her on the sofa, while Bertie shuffled his feet and looked defiant.

'Well, now, Aunt Lyddie. I understand that Bertie has been falsely accused of getting this Mildred Price into trouble. And before we go any further, I'd like your assurance that you've had no part in this, Bertie.'

'Why does everybody keep asking me that?' Bertie burst out. 'How many more times? I took the wretched girl out and kissed her once or twice, and that's all.'

Charles raised a hand.

'I just have to be sure of all the facts, Bertie. Now, that being the case, why do you suppose she picked on you?'

Bertie shrugged.

'No doubt the chap who got her in this hole has done a bunk, leaving her high and dry.'

A thought occurred to Lydia

'I suppose the chit really is in an interesting condition? Isn't there some way we can find out?'

'What does it matter, Mother?' Paula frowned. 'That won't tell us who the father is.'

'No,' Lydia said, looking up at Charles. 'But suppose this is all a swindle, and that Price man is in on it.'

'In what way, Aunt Lyddie?'

'Well, my clever son has boasted about his future inheritance and the girl has gone home and told her father all about it. Together they hatch a little plan to relieve Bertie of his money. The girl probably isn't in an interesting condition at all.'

Bertie leaned forward eagerly.

'That makes sense, Charles. After all, they can't have expected me to leap into marriage with the girl, when I know I'm innocent. As Ma said, they must want to blackmail us. If I don't pay up they'll spread all kinds of lies. I don't much care for myself. It's Ma I'm thinking of.'

And what about her, Paula asked herself. Did nobody care what happened to her reputation?

'All this supposition is getting us nowhere,' Charles said. 'I shall act at once. If you'll provide me with the correct address, Bertie, I shall dispatch a stern letter, warning these people that if they persist in their demands we shall sue them for slander.'

'No, Charles!' Lydia protested. 'We must avoid that! I couldn't bear to see our name in the newspapers.'

'With luck the mere threat will be

enough, Aunt Lyddie. If not, I shall have no hesitation in informing the police. Blackmail is a serious crime.'

Paula hoped he was right. There was one flaw in her cousin's argument. If Millie had lied to her father and he truly believed that Bertie was responsible for his daughter's condition, then he wouldn't give up easily.

Later, sitting on a rustic seat in the garden, Paula was pleased when Charles came and sat beside her. Her mother had lain down, pleading headache, and Bertie had disappeared.

'Charles, how could this have happened? It's so awful!'

'Be thankful for small mercies. At least Bertie's inheritance is safe until he's twenty-five, and your grandfather had the trust tied up so tightly that no amount of trying can break it.'

'I've never understood. Why does Bertie have to wait until he's twenty-five, when he came of age last year? Isn't it usual to get one's money at twenty-one?'

'Your grandfather was a very wise man, Paula. He wanted to make sure that his wealth would survive to be handed down through the generations, so he set up a trust, for the benefit of his son and grandson. I suppose he hoped that Bertie would have sown his wild oats by his mid-twenties.'

Charles laughed, but Paula didn't find this amusing. Knowing Bertie as she did, it was all too probable that the money would slip through his fingers like water from a tap.

Since leaving school Bertie had started one job or another, only to throw each one up after a few weeks because he found them boring.

'Have you thought about your own position, Paula?'

'I don't know what you mean.'

'At present, as his widow, your mother receives an income from your father's estate. As her daughter you, of course, live under her roof. When the estate passes to your brother, he will be responsible for supporting you both.'

Paula's mouth went dry. It was unbearable to think that she could be dependent on the whims of her younger brother! She jumped to her feet and muttered that it was time she went indoors.

That evening Lydia seemed determined to put away all thoughts of trouble to come, and embarked on polite conversation instead.

'Charles, tell us what you're doing with yourself these days in Gloucester. I suppose you play cricket, perhaps?'

'I do, but I'm taking time off to go to Canada.'

'Canada! What on earth for?'

'I'm going to a place called Calgary to join my fiancée.'

'You're engaged to be married? Who is she? How did you meet her? What do her parents do?'

'Her name is Lola King. Well, Laurena, actually.'

'How sweet.'

'We met in Switzerland when I was there for the skiing last winter, and we came to know each other quite well. Her father is in Calgary on business and Mrs King and Lola have gone with him. It's a frontier town and they thought I'd like to see a bit of the Wild West while they're staying there. I shall travel back to England with them, and then we'll start making plans for the wedding.'

Paula blinked back hot tears. She ought to be glad for him, but how could she be? Oh, she'd always known in the back of her mind that he would marry some day, but now that it was about to happen it had come as a dreadful shock. It felt like the end of her world.

The Hunt For Bertie

'Elsie! This toast is cold! Kindly fetch some hot and put this in the bin for the pig man.'

Hearing her mother's complaining voice Paula hurried towards the morning room.

'There you are, dear!' Mrs Scott pouted. 'Shall I pour your tea?'

'Thank you, Mother. Bertie not down yet?'

'No, I expect he's having a lie-in.'

Lucky for some, Paula thought. This was her busiest day of the week. Because she was a freelance teacher, visiting her pupils in their own homes, she naturally had to see them outside of regular school hours. She smiled wryly.

'What are you smiling at, Paula? I hope you're not rejoicing in poor Bertie's misfortune.'

Paula came to with a start.

'Of course not, Mother, but I do think you might be a bit more firm with him. He can't go through life throwing up perfectly good jobs just because he gets bored.'

'He just hasn't found anything worthy of his talents.'

'What talents?' Paula muttered.

The smell of burned toast filled the air.

'Really!' Lydia snapped. 'What on earth is the matter with that girl this morning? At this rate we'll be out of bread and the baker doesn't call today.'

'I think she's rattled because of that business yesterday. That horrid man wasn't very nice to her.'

'It's poor Bertie who ought to be upset, my girl.'

Paula had no wish to embark on another long discussion about the wicked Millie and her father, so she stood up.

'I'm sorry, Mother; I'll have to go. The Pilkingtons are expecting me and I mustn't be late. It's Mrs Pilkington.

Her husband plays the violin and she wants to learn to play the piano so she can accompany him.'

'Oh. Well, have a nice day, dear.'

But somehow the gods who arrange nice days were not looking after Paula that day. Mrs Pilkington collapsed into tears after being shown the basics and, hearing her raised voice, her husband rushed to her defence.

'Oh, Edward! I know I'll never be able to do this!'

'Then you mustn't go on with it,' her husband told her. 'Really, Miss Scott! There was no need to be unkind. My poor wife was only trying to please me by taking these totally unnecessary lessons.'

'But I wasn't. I was just . . . ' Mariah Pilkington gazed up at her husband, looking pitiful. 'Oh, darling, I just thought that I could accompany you instead of that blonde woman who goes with you everywhere.'

Paula saw it all now. Jealousy was at work here! Was the woman simply suffering from a newlywed's lack of self-confidence, or was something going on between Darling Edward and his accompanist?

'That will be all, Miss Scott,' the man said firmly as his wife sobbed on his shoulder. 'You need not come again.'

Moments later Paula found herself on the doorstep, fuming. In her agitation she hadn't asked for her money. She strongly suspected that the woman hadn't wanted to take lessons at all, and the scene she'd made had been to get a message across to her husband.

Next stop was the Rowse establishment.

'Papa says I can have fencing lessons!' Philip enthused.

Paula's heart sank.

'Instead of learning to play the piano?'

'Well, sort of. He says if I pass the first examination, then I can stop, and do fencing instead. He says that people should finish what they start.'

Philip sat down at the piano and

rattled off his scales in fine style. After that he went through the simple pieces she had assigned him with only one or two mistakes. In short, his performance was the best he had ever achieved.

'Well done, Philip! You must have practiced hard.'

The child beamed.

'Yes, miss. Do you think I'll pass the examination?'

Paula sighed.

'You've a long way to go yet, Philip, but if you carry on like this then, yes, I'm sure you'll succeed.'

Another pupil down the drain, she thought, as she marched off to her next lesson. Mr Rowse had succeeded in motivating his son, but it was to Paula's disadvantage.

The house was quiet when Paula reached home that afternoon. There was no sign of Mother, and no evidence of tea being prepared. Surely it wasn't Elsie's afternoon off? Her stomach rumbling, she opened the kitchen door, meaning to make herself a sandwich.

'Elsie! What on earth is the matter?' she cried, finding Elsie dabbing at her face with a wet handkerchief.

'Oh, Miss Paula! Your ma's given me the sack!'

'Just let me put the kettle on, Elsie. And I want something to eat. What have we got to put in a sandwich?'

'We've a nice bit of ham, and there's some cold beef, but there ain't no bread. I burned the last of it this morning, and that's what got your ma in an uproar.'

Paula frowned.

'Where is Mother now, Elsie?'

'Upstairs. Lying down with one of her heads. I wouldn't advise you to go up there, not with the mood she's in.'

'And my brother? Where is he? Not still in bed, I hope?'

Elsie began to wail.

'Shush! Do you want to waken Mother?'

Preserve me from howling women, she thought. Paula rummaged in the larder and found the remains of a fruitcake in the tin. When the pair of them had emptied the teapot she looked Elsie in the eye.

'Now, tell me straight what has happened to Bertie.'

Elsie sniffed.

'Well, miss, when he didn't come down to breakfast I waited. So she tells me, just go up to Mr Bertie's room and knock on the door. Well, I do that, miss; but no answer, so I opens the door and there's nobody there. There is a note on the pillow. *Staying with friends. Don't worry. Bertie.*

'I take it to the missus, and she has one of her turns, and I think I should get them pills of hers, only I can't find them. 'Get out,' she says, 'you're useless. And don't come back.' So that's what happened, and I don't know what to do now. I've no place to go.' The tears began to flow again.

Paula patted her on the back,

'Cheer up, Elsie! I'll sort all this out. You get your hat on, and go out for a nice walk in the park.'

Up in her room Paula tore off her hat and sank down on the bed. Curse all brothers, and curse all music students! On the way home she'd made up her mind to stop giving lessons. But now she began to question her decision. Did she really want to spend the rest of her life under Mother's roof? But there were not many positions open to women in 1912. There was school-teaching, of course; but she wasn't qualified for that, unless it was possible to obtain a position of music teacher in a boarding-school for young ladies. Of course, one would never meet men in such an environment. She would like to be married some day, but at twenty-five years of age she was dangerously close to being on the shelf, as Mother never tired of telling her.

* * *

'He's gone, I tell you! Bertie has gone!' Lydia wailed loudly.

'I don't suppose he's gone far,

Mother. And perhaps it's for the best that he's not here for the moment. Cousin Charles is on his way back to Gloucester and he'll put a letter in the post first thing on Monday morning. Those Prices will get their comeuppance and this business will soon die down.'

'My poor boy! Driven out of his own home!'

'He's hardly a boy, Mother. He's a grown man. I expect he's having a high old time with an old school chum.'

Lydia sniffed.

'This dreadful accusation! Bertie is completely innocent, you know.'

'Of course he is, Mother.'

But inside Paula's head a little voice suggested that Bertie might not be as innocent as he made out. If he had nothing to fear, why run away? But then, that was Bertie all over. Why face unpleasantness if one didn't have to?

One morning, about a month after Bertie had left, the postman delivered a letter.

‘Here’s one with a funny stamp, Miss,’ Elsie said, as she stooped to pick up a blue envelope from the doormat.

‘Let me see that, Elsie, please.’ Paula noted with a sinking feeling that the handwriting was Bertie’s. Putting her thumb under the flap she tore the letter open.

‘’Ere, Miss! That letter is addressed to your ma. You won’t half cop it, opening someone else’s post.’

Paula was more concerned with keeping bad news from her mother. Once she knew the worst she could break it to the older woman gently.

The note was short and to the point.

I’m here in Calgary, Alberta, Canada. There are lots of cowboys and Indians. Hope I don’t get scalped. Ha! Ha! Looking for a job. Don’t worry about me. Love, Bertie.

‘It’s from my brother. He’s gone to Canada.’

Elsie’s mouth dropped open.

‘Whatever for? Is it because of that Mr Price, then?’

'All I know is that Mother is going to be very upset when she hears about this.'

'Oh, yes, miss! I hope this doesn't kill her, I'm sure. I remember when my Aunt Ethel got the news about my cousin in the Navy falling overboard off his ship, and . . . '

Paula never did find out what happened to Aunt Ethel, because at that moment she heard Lydia calling her from upstairs.

'Was that the postman I heard? Any news of Bertie?'

'I think you'd better sit down, Mother. Yes, I've received a letter from him. Shall I read it to you?'

Paula had to read it aloud twice before the news really sunk in. Her poor mother stared up at her in bewilderment.

'Calgary? But that's where Charles is going, isn't it?'

'Perhaps that's where Bertie got hold of the idea.'

'But why has Bertie gone there?'

'Perhaps he wants to be a cowboy,' Paula rejoined, hoping to diffuse the situation with a bit of humour.

'Why should he? He can't even ride a horse.'

Paula couldn't bear to watch her mother weeping into a tiny lace handkerchief, so she crept out of the room.

However, later that day Lydia bustled into the sitting-room, seemingly fully recovered.

'I've made up my mind, Paula,' she announced. 'Canada is no place for Bertie. Someone will have to go to this Calgary place and bring the boy home.'

'You mean Cousin Charles? But even if he does find Bertie he can't be expected to bring him home, just like that. He's meant to be travelling with Miss King, isn't he?'

'Then you shall go, Paula. It's most convenient that you've decided to give up this nonsense of going out and about to give piano lessons. It isn't suitable for a young woman in your position. I've made up my mind, Paula. You have nothing else to do. You shall go to Canada.'

Lydia beamed at her daughter, obviously enjoying the role of fairy godmother. Cinderella may have relished the idea of going to the ball in all her glory, but Paula wasn't so sure about this.

'Ships are not very safe,' she quavered. 'I don't much like the idea of going to sea.' It was only a matter of weeks since the terrible tragedy of the *Titanic* had occurred, and that was enough to give anyone pause.

'Of course, that was absolutely dreadful,' Lydia agreed, 'but it won't happen again, will it? You'll be quite safe.'

'I'm a single woman, Mother. How can I travel alone, staying in hotels, perhaps, completely unchaperoned? What about my reputation?'

Lydia paused. Then, suddenly, her face lit up.

'Cousin Charles! You can travel with

him. You'll be quite safe then!'

'Why don't you come, Mother? A sea voyage would do you good.'

'Have you gone mad? Charles says that this Calgary place is a frontier town, probably full of gamblers and women of ill repute. It's no place for a woman like me!'

'Nor me,' Paula wanted to say, but she bit back the words. Attempting to stop Lydia in full flow was like trying to stop salmon swimming upstream to spawn.

Paula needed to think. On one hand Bertie had got himself into a muddle. Let him sort himself out, or suffer the consequences. On the other hand, why shouldn't she do as her mother asked? That evening she sat in her bedroom, massaging the tense muscles in her neck. It would be an adventure.

The expedition would also call for a new wardrobe. She had read in a magazine that people dressed for dinner on board ship. She only possessed one evening gown, an out of date garment she'd worn for her twenty-first birthday celebration. That certainly wouldn't do. She would let Mother know that she'd be letting Cousin Charles down if she travelled with him dressed like a country cousin.

She expected Lydia to have changed her tune before morning, but if anything she was even more determined.

'I'm about to send Elsie to the post office,' she said. 'I've drafted a telegram to Cousin Charles. What do you think of this? Paula to accompany you to Canada, stop. Bertie already there, stop. Please make all arrangements, stop. Letter following, stop.'

She looked expectantly at Paula.

'Well? What do you think?'

'What do I think? For a start, we'd better not mention Bertie. You know what Miss Evans at the post office is like. The news will be all over Wimbledon before lunchtime. And if Joshua Price gets to hear about it, he's bound to think that it's a sign of Bertie's guilt. He'll be down on us like an avenging angel, Mother.'

'Hmm. I suppose you're right. Cross that bit out, then.'

'I'm not sure I want everyone knowing that I'm going to the other side of the world with a man, either, Mother.'

'Don't be silly, dear. Charles is your cousin.'

'Charles is no relation to me. None at all.'

'Perhaps not, but Gladys Evans doesn't know that. You've nothing to fear from him, Paula. He's an engaged man, crossing the Atlantic to meet the woman he intends to marry.'

But Paula knew that she had everything to fear. She had loved Charles Ingram all her life. First as a little girl, looking up to him as a hero, and then as a girl in her teens, caught up in her first romance, even though he'd never known of it.

Now that love had somehow grown deeper, but sadly it was all to no avail. He was going to marry Lola, and that was the end of that.

On Board

September. Paula could hardly believe how majestic the great Cunard steamship was. She had seen pictures, of course, but no painting on a brochure could do justice to its magnificence in real life. Once on board she trotted along in Charles's wake, trying to look as if she crossed the Atlantic on a regular basis, instead of this being what Lydia referred to as her maiden voyage.

'I hope they take good care of my luggage,' she murmured, when Charles turned to ask her how she was. 'I hated leaving it back there unattended.'

'Don't worry about a thing,' he assured her. 'You did put the proper sticker on your trunk, I assume, so that it will end up in the hold?'

'*Not Wanted On Voyage*. Yes, I did. Oh, Charles, this is all so overwhelming. There are so many passageways and decks. I'm sure I'll get lost.'

'You'll catch on. Besides, you've me to look after you.'

But when she was settled in her cabin, Paula vowed that she would not follow Charles everywhere he went. She would do her best to amuse herself; perhaps even make friends with some of the other ladies on board. Her company had been more or less forced on him by Lydia.

As things turned out she saw more of Charles than she could have expected, for wherever she went, he usually turned up. Once she'd found her sea legs, as the captain put it, she tramped around the promenade deck every morning, before settling down on a chaise longue. Promptly at eleven o'clock each day a steward came along, dispensing consommé to the passengers. She wondered whether the passengers down in steerage received the same treatment.

'You're just in time,' she said, when Charles came and stretched out beside her. 'Although I'm surprised that anyone has room to eat in between meals. Hearty breakfasts, lunches and teas, with seven-course dinners to follow!'

'It's the sea air that gives one an appetite, Paula. Better make the most of it, because we won't be getting the same treatment in Canada, I'm sure. We'll be on the train for three or four days, Lola tells me.'

Lola! Paula had almost forgotten about her.

'I hope you've brought your glad rags,' Charles went on. 'There's to be dancing in the main saloon tomorrow night.'

'I think I'll just stay in my cabin and read. I've discovered the library here and they have books by my favourite authors. Besides, I shan't know anybody here.'

'Nonsense! You must come. And you certainly won't be a wallflower, my girl. I'm pretty good at tripping the light fantastic, if I do say so myself!'

That afternoon Paula set out to explore the ship. She turned into a passageway, following the sound of music. Someone was playing the piano, and doing it rather well. Peering around a door that stood ajar she caught a glimpse of an elderly man seated at a grand piano, skillfully completing a Beethoven sonata.

He glanced up as she hovered in the doorway.

'Come in, my dear. You enjoy music? Sit down beside me and I shall play for you. Do you care for Beethoven?'

'Very much.' Paula went forward, intrigued by this man. Who could he be? Perhaps he was one of the entertainers, employed by the Cunard Line?

Within moments she was swept away by music that left her breathless. He was playing the Appassionata Sonata, a work she had heard in person only once before, at a concert at the Albert Hall when a world-famous pianist was giving a rare performance.

'That was magnificent!' she blurted, when the flying fingers were still at last. 'Every bit as good as when I heard it at the Albert Hall last year.'

He smiled.

'Then I have not lost my touch.'

Paula was stunned. Could this possibly be the great Guido Rossi?

He waved away her stammered apologies.

'Great music is to be shared by all, my dear. Now, I think you shall play for me. You do play, do you not? You have the fingers of a pianist.'

'I couldn't! I mean, yes, I do play; I'm a children's piano teacher. But I couldn't possibly, really.'

'Do you know the Moonlight Sonata? I have the music here, you see. Please indulge an old man's whim. It is many years since a lovely girl has played for me. Not since my wife died, in fact.'

Trembling, Paula flexed her fingers and prepared to start. She stared at the sheet music with blurry eyes and then, suddenly, her inhibitions disappeared and her hands descended to the keys. Somehow she managed to get through the beautiful sonata without making a single mistake.

'Bravo, my dear! I can see that you have practiced long and well. Tell me more about yourself and your choice of this teaching career.'

Paula found herself explaining about her early dreams, which had come to nothing. He nodded in sympathy.

'It is not too late for you, my child. To perform as a solo artist on the international stage, that is a privilege given to only a few. But there are other ways in which you can make a contribution to the world, and your lessons for the little ones are but a beginning. Think about this, and you will find your way. Now, you must excuse me. I am an old man, and it is my bed that calls me.' He bowed, and left.

That evening a large number of people gathered in the same reception room for what was billed as a

Drawing-room Entertainment Night.

'In other words, Amateur Talent at the parish hall,' Charles said, rather sniffily, Paula thought, but in the event, he did accompany her.

'My goodness!' he exclaimed, when they were sitting in front-row seats. 'Do you see that distinguished-looking chap who's just come in? I could swear that's Guido Rossi! Surely it can't be the great man himself?'

'I suppose he travels like anybody else. Perhaps he has performances lined up in Canada.'

'I shouldn't think so. They say he retired when his wife died. She was the love of his life and he didn't want to go on without her.'

At that moment a roll of drums announced the start of the programme, and the master of ceremonies mounted the dais. Solos, recitations and a violin solo followed, all well received by the audience.

'And now, in conclusion, ladies and gentlemen, we have a wonderful treat in store. The world-renowned Signor Guido Rossi is in our midst, and he has kindly agreed to come down from First Class to play for us this evening.'

'I knew it was him,' Charles whispered, under cover of the hearty applause that followed.

The great man approached the piano.

'I am honoured to be asked to play for you tonight, ladies and gentlemen, but first, we have another treat in store. There is one among us who also loves the music of Beethoven, and I hope that I can persuade her to come forward to perform the Moonlight Sonata.' He waved his hand, palm uppermost, in Paula's direction.

Flustered, she turned to look behind her, but there was only the bar steward, standing there with a towel over his arm. The great man beckoned to her again.

'Come along, my dear.'

In a daze, Paula stepped forward, leaving Charles sitting bolt upright with his mouth open.

'I can't do this!' she hissed, when she reached the piano. 'Not in front of all these people!'

'Forget the audience. Play for me alone, my dear, just as you did earlier today.'

Gulping, Paula seated herself at the piano, arranging her skirts neatly over the stool. She smiled up at her mentor, lifted her hands, and became lost in the music.

Afterwards, returning to her place, she could hear the whispers.

'Who is she? A pupil of the great man, perhaps?'

It was obvious that Charles had a thousand questions to ask, but there was no time for talking because the sound of the Appassionata Sonata filled the room. Tumultuous applause followed Rossi's performance. The pianist simply smiled and bowed, and then marched out of the room. Into the silence there came a babble of voices as people commented on what they had seen and heard.

Having no wish to answer questions from this excited group Paula stood up and slipped out of the room.

* * *

'Where did you get to last night, Paula? I looked around but you'd gone.'

They were seated at the breakfast table, where Paula was toying with a plate of scrambled eggs.

'Come on, where on earth did you meet Signor Rossi? And I didn't know you could play like that. I thought you were just a . . . ' His voice trailed off.

'You thought I was just a little teacher, did you? Sitting quietly by while the children fumble through their scales? For your information, Charles Ingram, I once had dreams of performing on the concert stage.'

'I do seem to remember that, but I assumed it was a childhood whim.'

Paula hesitated.

'I believe it was Mother's dream, more than mine. I loved music from a very early age, but as somebody once said to me, I don't have that seed of greatness.'

'You still did jolly well last night,' Charles said. 'It will be something to tell Aunt Lydia about, won't it?'

'I might mention it when I write,' Paula agreed. To tell her mother face-to-face would be to unleash a flood of regrets and she could do without that. Meanwhile she had a lovely memory that would stay with her all her days.

Now, as she strolled along the promenade deck, she found that she was the centre of attention. Gentlemen lifted their hats in salute when they met; ladies smiled and nodded. One lady cornered her in the coffee room and actually called her Miss Rossi! They must think that she was Signor Rossi's daughter!

'My name is Miss Scott,' she explained. For a moment the woman appeared shocked, and then she recovered her aplomb. 'Then you are his daughter by a mistress? We must excuse such things in a great artiste, must we not?'

'I happen to be a music teacher from Wimbledon,' Paula snapped. 'My father was a university professor.'

Infuriated, Paula strode away, blundering into the Grand Saloon without noticing where she was going. In her flight she almost bumped into a steward carrying a tray.

'Steady on, miss, or you'll have me over! I say, I heard you play last night. I don't usually go in for that classical stuff, but you did all right.'

'Thank you. I'm glad you enjoyed it. And before you ask, I'm not Guido Rossi's daughter!'

'I never said you was, miss. I tell you what, though. If you're ever looking for a job, I bet they'd take you on here. They often have background music in the Palm Room and the like.'

'Thank you for the suggestion,' Paula murmured. 'I'll give it some thought.'

And think about it she did. Not that

Mother would approve! Paula could just see her face.

'A daughter of mine, working on a ship? That's no life for a lady, my girl. What would I tell my friends?'

Well, if Bertie could run away to become a cowboy, why shouldn't she play the piano on a ship? At least the passengers here would appreciate her efforts!

The most amazing side effect of Paula's triumph was the way in which Charles now viewed her.

'It's odd, but I'm seeing you differently after last night.'

'What a thing to say!'

'I've always thought of you as my little sister. I mean, I've known you since you were little more than a toddler. Now it looks as if I've never really known you at all.'

'There's nothing odd about that,' Paula rejoined, feeling awkward. 'It's true we spent most of our holidays together while we were growing up, but I daresay there's a great deal I don't know about you, either.'

'Then we must put that right, and what better time than now, when we've nothing to do until we dock at Quebec? You shall tell me your whole life story, Paula.'

'There isn't much to tell,' she said, laughing.

The dance that night was all that Paula could have hoped for. Luckily she had been sent to dancing class as a child, and she was fairly adept at the waltz, the foxtrot and the polka. As he had promised, Charles steered her around the floor in a perfectly acceptable fashion, but thanks to her brief moment of fame she didn't lack for partners. Under the subdued lighting her modestly priced evening gown looked as good as the garments worn by the more affluent ladies, and she was perfectly content.

'Ouch, it's hot in here!' Charles gasped, as they returned from dancing a Viennese waltz. 'Shall we go up on deck for a bit and get a breath of air?'

'If I can pop down to my cabin first. I'll need a wrap. It wouldn't do to arrive in Canada with a streaming cold.'

Gazing at the moonlight on the gently moving waves, Paula felt as if they were the only two people left in the world. Muted music in the background reminded her that, far away, the dancing was still going on, but that had a dream-like quality about it. She held her breath.

'Paula . . . ' Charles's voice was husky and low.

She waited. Then he took her in his arms and bent his head to hers. Lost in his kiss she knew that this man was her first love, and her only love. When at last he released her she swallowed hard and took a few steps backward.

'I'm so sorry, Paula. I hope I haven't offended you. I don't know what came over me. The music, the night air, the moonlight . . . '

'I'm not upset, but I do think we should go in now.'

Without speaking he escorted her to

her cabin, and then she heard the door of his own room shut firmly. She went inside and locked the door.

She caught sight of herself in the dressing-table mirror. Here was a young woman who had just received her first kiss. She should be looking radiant, but instead the golden-brown eyes held a hint of sadness.

Mother had warned her about shipboard romances.

'You may meet young men who amuse themselves by leading young women on, just to pass the time at sea. These little love affairs fade away like summer mist once the ship docks. So don't believe everything you hear.'

'No, Mother.'

'Of course, Cousin Charles will be there to protect you.'

Rather sadly, Paula had assumed that a shipboard romance was not for her. She was shy in male company and had no small talk. Instead she must be grateful for this marvellous holiday.

But now, everything was changed.

Bewitched by the moonlight, she and Charles had exchanged that passionate kiss, but that was all there could ever be between them. He belonged to another woman, and even now he was on his way to claim her as his bride. Mother was right. Soon the ship would dock and this beautiful interlude would be over.

The return voyage lay ahead of her, of course, but then Bertie would be with her.

An unhappy thought struck her. The Kings were supposed to be coming back to England soon. What if they, and of course Charles, travelled on the same ship as Paula and Bertie? She simply couldn't bear it if she had to watch the two lovebirds billing and cooing, as they surely would! She would have to lock herself in her cabin and plead a bad case of mal de mer!

But before there was any chance of that, the rest of the journey had to be got through. She understood that the train journey from Quebec City to

Calgary took four or five days.

'Why?' she'd questioned Charles. 'Does it keep stopping and starting or something?'

'Canada is a big country, Paula. It stretches almost four thousand miles from the Atlantic to the Pacific. We're not going all the way to the Pacific Ocean, of course, but quite far enough! Calgary is in Alberta, which was made into a province barely seven years ago. This is a young country, Paula, still in the process of being built.'

'Oh,' was all that Paula could think of to say in response to this piece of information.

The New World

Paula looked up and gasped. The ship had docked at Quebec City and now they were waiting to disembark. The object of Paula's awe was a magnificent, fairytale turreted castle.

'That's the Château Frontenac,' Charles said, looking over her shoulder. 'Isn't it something?'

'It certainly is! Who on earth lives there, Charles?'

'Nobody. That is, it was never someone's home. It's a hotel, built about twenty years ago, as a stopover place for passengers on the Canadian Pacific Railway. We're going to be staying there, actually. Apparently it's built on the site of an old château.'

Paula hardly listened. She was too busy admiring the opulence of the CPR hotel, which she suspected might be their last sight of civilization for some time to come. She'd heard that Calgary was a frontier town, which conjured up visions of rowdy men and unpaved streets. For the first time she felt glad that Charles was with her to keep her safe.

Being on terra firma felt strange, and once or twice she stumbled, unable to adjust her stride from the seaman's roll she had developed on board ship. She longed to go and lie down, but on arriving at the hotel they were told that their rooms were not yet ready. Departure time was at midday, and previous guests had until then to vacate their rooms. In the meantime, why not take part in a guided tour of the sights of Quebec?

This they did, Charles agreeing that it would be too bad to miss out on the opportunity. With Paula's hand tucked into Charles's supporting arm they walked on the Plains of Abraham where British General James Wolfe had perished in 1759 in the decisive battle against the French.

'There was a painting of Wolfe's death in my school history book,' Paula said. 'To think I'm actually standing on the spot where he died! Or close to it, at any rate.'

'When we go into the Old Town you'll see the Cathedral of the Holy Trinity,' Charles said, referring to a guidebook he'd purchased. 'I want to see that.'

Charles shook his head, explaining that it was modelled on St Martin's In The Fields, a famous church in London's Trafalgar Square, and therefore well worth viewing.

Indeed, it was quite lovely inside. As they emerged, a petite white-haired lady nudged Paula's elbow and asked in a loud whisper whether they were on their honeymoon.

Paula blushed.

'Oh, no. I'm with my cousin. We're just travelling together on our way to seeing my brother.'

'Going west, are you?'

'Just as far as Calgary.'

'Ah. My husband and I are only going as far as Ottawa. That's the capital, you know.'

Paula did know. Not for nothing had their schoolmistress drilled into them the names of the capitals of the world. And Canada was part of the Empire! It would be a poor Briton who knew nothing of its geography and history.

As she and Charles walked through the old cobbled streets she admired all the grey stone buildings, making up stories in her head about the people who lived there. All French-Canadian, she supposed, although their tour guide had told them that, long ago, soldiers had been billeted in private homes as part of the British garrison. She wondered what the housewives had thought about that. She hoped they'd been paid for their trouble.

She hardly slept that night. Her bed was comfortable but now that they were safely on Canadian soil she had begun to worry. This was a huge country, and there was no telling where, in its vastness, her brother might be. His note had said that he was in Calgary, but what if he had moved on?

In the morning, when they were breakfasting on buttermilk pancakes slathered in maple syrup, she confided these fears to Charles, who laughed them off.

'Bertie is a grown man. If he can't look after himself at his age, I fear for his future!'

'But that's not the point, Charles! Mother is trusting me to find him and bring him safely home.'

'The boy has to cut loose from her apron strings sooner or later, and I'm sure he won't thank Aunt Lydia for sending his sister to drag him home like a schoolboy. In fact, I'm surprised at you for going along with her plan.'

'I suppose I liked the idea of cutting myself free from Mama's apron strings, too.' Paula gave him a wry smile. 'I've always wanted to travel, but I never dreamed I'd cross the Atlantic in a Cunard liner! This is the holiday of a lifetime for me, but it does come with responsibilities attached. What if I can't reach up to her expectations? I don't know how I'll be able to face her.'

'You're acting as if this muddle is all your fault. Bertie is to blame, if anyone is. Besides, I'm here to help you. Mr King will have contacts. He should be able to steer us in the right direction. And of course the North West Mounted Police will have all sorts of resources.'

'Not the police, Charles. Poor Mother would have a fit!'

Charles patted her on the hand.

'Stop worrying, Paula! It's almost time for us to board the train, and we've an exciting few days to look forward to as we cross the country. There may be grizzly bears and buffalo, for example. Just think of all the exciting tales you'll have to tell when you return to Wimbledon.'

Wimbledon. It seemed years away, and right at this moment Paula didn't care if she never saw it again! She longed to continue this happy dream she inhabited, even though she knew that Charles Ingram would not be part of it for very much longer.

The first thing that Paula noticed about their point of departure was that, unlike English stations, it didn't have platforms. At least, there were low wooden walkways alongside the rails, but they were not built in such a fashion as to reach up to the doors of the waiting train. She prayed that her narrow skirt would not hobble her as she tried to climb up, or worst of all, split wide open! However, as the clock struck nine several of the doors opened and uniformed men let down sets of portable steps. With Charles's hand on her elbow she negotiated these quite handily and was soon settled in her seat.

'Will my trunk be all right?' she fretted.

'Of course it will. Do stop worrying! And even if it does go astray, it wouldn't be the end of the world. I'm sure they have dress shops in Calgary!'

* * *

Despite the new surroundings and the different people to observe, Paula found the train journey tedious. At times the scenery was sensational, but she discovered that she couldn't stare out of the window for long periods without getting restless. They were given some relief each time they arrived at some sizeable place; the train stopped and the passengers were allowed to get off and walk about.

She heard a woman complain to her husband about this.

'There's nothing to see here, Joseph! Just a lot of common sheds and factory buildings. I expected to see shops, and some nice houses. Where are they all?'

'This is a railroad station, Amelia. Obviously it's been built on the edge of town because the folks in those nice houses, as you call them, wouldn't want to hear all the noise and shunting. Besides, these factories need to be close to the tracks, see, so they can get their goods to market.'

Amelia wasn't appeased. She turned to Paula, pouting.

'I don't know as I can stand much more of this! For two pins I'd turn around right now and get back home to Halifax. Don't you feel the same?'

'I'm afraid it wouldn't be that easy for me,' Paula told her. 'I've come all the way from England, you see.'

'Oh, my! Now, that's what I'd like to do. See England. That your hubby back there, is it? Such a handsome man. I saw you sitting together on the train. Newlyweds, are you? On your honeymoon?'

'That's my cousin.'

She could almost see the wheels turning in the woman's brain. Scarlet woman! Travelling alone with a man!

'My brother is in Calgary, and I'm going to join him there. My cousin is going to the same place to join his fiancée, so my mother thought we should travel together.'

'Oh, yes?' The woman still didn't

seem convinced, looking Paula up and down with narrowed eyes.

'Charles and I practically grew up together,' Paula babbled on. 'We're quite like brother and sister.'

Why she should care what this person thinks was beyond her. Once they got off this train they would never see each other again, and good riddance.

But in that she was mistaken.

Back on the train she tried to make conversation with Charles. Needing to prepare herself for their inevitable separation, she quizzed him about his fiancée's family.

'I don't think you've ever told me just why they are staying in Calgary. What does Mr King do for a living?'

'He's a high-powered business executive,' Charles muttered, briefly looking up from the newspaper he'd bought at the station kiosk.

Well, now she knew! Mr King was a high-powered business executive, whatever that was!

'But what does he actually do for a living?'

'Hmm? Oh, he's in oil, I think, among other things.'

'Boiling?' Paula asked, giggling.

With a sigh he folded his paper and turned to face her.

'Look, Paula, if you're still fretting about what will happen when we get to Calgary, you've absolutely no need to worry. I shan't desert you. Lola's mother is sure to know of places to stay and I'm sure she'll be happy to take you under her wing. Why, she may even invite you to stay with them. I understand that they've taken quite a large house.'

'I wouldn't want to impose.'

'You're part of my family, Paula. I'm sure they'll do everything they can to make you feel safe in the city.'

'A city? You've been calling it a frontier town!'

'It's a bit of both, I think. The North West Mounted Police built a fort there in 1875, and things started to hum after the Canadian Pacific Railway arrived in 1883. Calgary became a city a few years after that. As far as I can gather there's still more than a bit of the Wild West about it. I'm sure that Bertie will get his fill of cowboys!'

'And does Lola enjoy that sort of thing? Bucking broncos and handsome cowboys?'

Charles laughed.

'Lola is a very ladylike creature, more concerned with the latest fashions from Paris and attending soirées.'

'You won't live in Calgary when you're married, then?'

'Of course not. I've a law practice to return to in Gloucester, in case you've forgotten. I've no doubt that Calgary will become a thriving metropolis some day, but in the meantime my life is set on a certain course and I must follow that.'

'Yes,' Paula agreed sadly. 'I shall miss you, Charles. So will Mother, but I suppose that everything has to change as life goes on.'

'Nonsense! You'll see more of me than ever, once we're settled. Lola will wish to go to London on a regular basis and I know she'll want to see more of you. She'll be the sister you've never had, Paula. Won't that be fun?'

'Um.' She looked down at her hands. 'I'm feeling a bit sleepy. I think I'll have a nap.'

'Good idea, old girl.' Charles unfolded his paper and was soon engrossed in the headlines.

Paula's heart was heavy. If she and Lola took a liking to each other, she would be honour bound to show the other girl the sights of London. Charles would never understand if she snubbed his future wife. But how could she bear it when Lola shared all her hopes for the future?

For one wild moment she toyed with the idea of telling Charles what was in her heart. Sadly, she accepted the fact that it would do more harm than good. He would recoil from Paula, telling her that all she felt was a schoolgirl crush.

And perhaps it was a silly crush, for what sensible woman would allow herself to fall for an engaged man?

Paula awakened with a start as the uniformed conductor strode down the aisle, calling, ‘Calgary in five minutes! Calgary in five minutes!’

All around her people stood up, beginning to retrieve their belongings from the overheard racks. In a very short time they would have reached their destination and a chapter in Paula’s life would have closed for ever.

The Stampede

They were met at the station by a uniformed chauffeur in an open motor-car. She had never ridden in one before and even though she was sitting in the back seat she felt particularly vulnerable, especially when they came too close to a passing carriage and the horse reared in fright. There were people everywhere.

'Why don't they stay off the road?' Paula squawked, when they came close to hitting a couple in front of the car.

'It's the Stampede, Miss,' the chauffeur explained.

She wondered what that meant. She looked at the passing scenery with interest. Many of the buildings, including the houses, seemed to be made of wood. Some of the shops seemed to have false fronts, apparently to make them appear larger and more prosperous than they really were. These façades reached up as though part of another storey, yet the building consisted of just the ground floor.

After some time they came to what must be a more affluent residential area. The architecture was different and some were constructed of brick or stone. The Kings' rented house was one of the finest, set back behind some well-kept shrubbery.

Charles rang the doorbell and they were admitted by a uniformed maid. A petite blonde girl came racing down the stairs, almost knocking Charles off his feet when she flung herself into his arms.

'Darling, how wonderful to see you! I thought you'd never get here. How was the journey? Was it very dreadful? You must come and say hello to Mama! She's put off making calls this morning so she can greet you properly.'

Obviously this was the lovely Lola.

'Steady on, darling; you'll have me over,' Charles murmured, holding the girl at arm's length after kissing her cheek. 'There's someone I'd like you to meet. Paula, as you will have gathered this is my fiancée, Lola King. Lola, this is my cousin, Paula Scott.'

'How do you do.'

'You didn't tell us she was coming,' Lola said, ignoring Paula's outstretched hand.

Paula wilted under Lola's critical gaze. If this was a sample of her future cousin's manners, she didn't think much of them!

Fortunately the maid returned a moment later, saying that Sir and Madam requested their presence in the drawing-room. Trying to clamp down on her growing annoyance Paula followed Charles and Lola. Mrs King, a stout lady in a burgundy-coloured dress, had what was known in fashion circles as a pouter-pigeon bosom, glistening with a sparkling necklace. Her husband was equally rotund but much taller. His white hair and matching moustache gave him an air of dignity.

Introductions were made.

'My cousin and I travelled to Canada together,' Charles explained. 'She has come to Calgary to meet her brother.'

Mrs King looked relieved.

'Where is your brother staying, Miss Scott? Will he be coming here to collect you, or shall you go to his hotel? I expect you'd like to go and tidy up first, and then we'll serve luncheon. Afterwards we'll be happy to lend you our car to take you wherever you wish to go. I do hope we shall see something of you during your stay in Calgary, although unfortunately our social calendar is rather heavily booked for the month of September. If only we had known you were coming we could have made other arrangements. Charles is very naughty not to have let us know. Ah, well, I expect his head was so full of thoughts of getting together again with Lola that he completely forgot about you!'

Lola simpered.

Now came the moment of truth.

'I'm afraid we don't quite know where Bertram is. Aunt Lydia felt it opportune that I was coming to Canada at the same time and able to escort Paula.'

Samuel King nodded his approval.

'Quite right, too! I'd feel the same if our little Lola had to travel abroad.'

'The fact is,' Charles went on, less sure of his ground now, 'Paula has to find a place to stay until Bertie turns up. Perhaps you can suggest a suitable hotel, Mrs King, or, failing that, a respectable boarding-house.'

Samuel King let out a great guffaw, startling Paula.

'You wouldn't find anywhere with a cupboard to let, much less a room, my boy! Everywhere has been booked up for months. It's the Stampede, you see!'

There it was again — the Stampede, whatever that was. Paula looked at Charles, who was obviously taken aback.

'I'm sorry, we had no idea,' he said. 'I should have thought, but what with one thing and another . . . '

Silence engulfed the room. His future father-in-law recovered first.

'Why, there's no problem at all, my boy. Miss Scott can stay here, can't she, Beatrice?'

His wife's face was a study.

'We've the Berkeleys coming this weekend, Samuel.'

'So what? We've more than enough rooms. If we don't, then I'm sure Miss Scott won't mind pigging it with Lola! All girls together, eh?'

Lola shot a look of such venom at the other girl that Paula wished the floor would open and swallow her up. It was her own fault; she should have made arrangements for a place to stay instead of depending on finding Bertie and sharing his accommodation.

As Paula came downstairs after a hasty wash, she met Charles coming up.

'I'm so embarrassed!' she hissed.

'No need to be. It's all settled, and I know that Lola is delighted to have you here.'

It was obvious that he hadn't noticed the expression on Lola's face. Was she jealous of Paula, or was it simply that she wanted all the attention for herself? First thing in the morning Paula would make the rounds of all the places where Bertie might be, then she would thank the Kings for their hospitality and leave their house with a sigh of relief.

'What is this stampede I keep hearing about?' she asked Mr King, when she found herself seated at his right hand during luncheon.

'Rough men doing idiotic things on horses and cows,' Lola snapped, passing a dish of green beans to Charles.

'Not cows, girl,' her father corrected. 'Bulls.'

Lola shrugged. Her father turned back to Paula.

'We've just had the summer exhibition, and many folks will be staying on for the Stampede. It's partly a Wild West show and rodeo event, but there will be horse-racing as well. All the best cowboys will be here from across

Canada, America and Mexico. There's to be bull-riding, street-wrestling, tie-down roping and bareback riding.'

'What did I tell you!' Lola muttered.

'We're all going to see the Grand Parade tomorrow,' Beatrice King remarked. 'We've taken a viewing box in the show arena, right next to the Royal Box. The Duke of Connaught and Princess Patricia will be in attendance. We may even meet them.'

Paula brightened at this. Bertie would most certainly be somewhere among the crowd, drawn there by all the cowboy antics. After that, everything would be fine.

When she spoke to Samuel King, he shook his head.

'According to this morning's 'Herald' there are more than 80,000 people in town at present. It wouldn't be safe for you to go wandering around. I'd never forgive myself if anything happened to you. Charles will help seek the lad out, won't you, my boy?'

His wife was in agreement with him,

pointing out that Paula could get hurt in the crush of spectators.

Lola looked as if she could eat nails, Paula wrote in her journal that night. If she doesn't watch out, Charles will see through her, although I must say that he seems completely besotted at the moment.

* * *

The next day, viewing the Grand Parade from the wooden box, Paula was thankful that she had listened to her hosts and come with them to the exhibition ground. For one thing, they had a splendid view of what was happening at ground level. For another, she was amazed by the huge surging crowds of people who were in attendance. The numbers were far more than she had anticipated. If Bertie did happen to be down there somewhere she would never be able to find him.

She knew she'd never forget the parade. First came a splendid band, led by a burly man carrying an enormous drum. The men who came after him marched in precision, playing brass instruments that shone in the sun.

'Here comes the Duke now!' Mrs King enthused, leaning forward in her seat. 'He's a royal duke, of course, Prince Arthur, Queen Victoria's third son.'

'Of course, he's Canada's Governor General now, as of last year,' Mr King explained. 'And that's his daughter with him, the Princess Patricia.'

The royal pair were riding in a landau, surrounded by members of the Mounted Police in their colourful uniforms. The princess was all in white.

Dozens of open carriages followed the royal landau, carrying attendants and local dignitaries, Paula supposed. Then came all sorts of people on horseback. Some appeared to be soldiers in dress uniforms while others, judging by their homespun attire were probably cowboys. Splendidly attired native people followed after them, some riding and others on foot. The skirl of bagpipes reached Paula's ears as a kilted pipe band hove into view, reminding the watchers that in the pioneer days Canada had been settled by thousands of Scots.

It took almost half an hour for the parade to pass in front of them. After a pause for the dignitaries to settle in their seats, the competitions would begin.

Suddenly, with a low moan Lola crumpled to the floor. Lola's face was turned away from everyone but Paula, who noticed that the girl's eyes opened wide for a moment in an alert, calculating glance.

'I don't know what happened,' she heard Lola say in a weak voice.

'I have my smelling salts here,' Mrs King said. 'Take a good sniff, Lola.'

'There's no need, Mama. I'll be all right now.'

'Nonsense! We'll take you home and call for the doctor.'

'I don't need a doctor, Mama, but I

think it will be best if I go home.'

'Of course, darling. We'll all come with you.'

'That won't be necessary. Charles will take me home, won't you, darling?' Lola gazed up at him.

Paula groaned inwardly. Lola had engineered this very nicely. Now she would have him all to herself for the day, keeping unwanted cousins at bay. Perhaps that was fair enough, they were an engaged couple, after all. But surely Charles could see that he was being manipulated?

'How long do you mean to stay, Miss Scott?' Mrs King asked, when her daughter had disappeared.

Paula swallowed hard.

'I suppose until you are ready to leave, Mrs King. I'm not sure if I could find my way back to the house on foot.'

'That wasn't quite what I meant. I do feel that the young couple should be given time alone, don't you?'

'Of course, Mrs King. I'm most grateful for the hospitality I've been given. As soon as I find my brother I shall leave. Charles has placed an advertisement in the personal column of 'The Herald'.'

'You must, of course, stay with us for as long as you wish,' her husband said, with a frown at his wife.

'Thank you, Mr King. You are so kind,' Paula murmured.

The next morning, immediately after breakfast, she announced that she was returning to the exhibition ground where some of the rodeo events were to take place.

'Good idea,' Charles said, wiping his lips with his linen napkin. 'We'll come with you.'

'Oh, no, darling,' Lola chimed in. 'I don't think I should go out among all those crowds in this heat.'

'Perhaps you're wise, Lola. You won't mind if I go, then, will you? It seems a shame to come all this way from England and not see a marvellous spectacle like this.'

'I want you with me,' Lola pouted.

But Charles turned a deaf ear to her blandishments.

'I missed everything yesterday to stay with you, Lola, and of course I was glad to do so. However, I don't want to miss this, and you'll be well taken care of here.'

Samuel King nodded in agreement.

'That's right. Off you go and enjoy yourself.'

'Are you sure you won't come?' Charles asked.

'Quite sure, thank you! You won't need me when you have Miss Scott hanging on your every word!' Lola turned and flounced out of the room.

Paula decided that she wouldn't like to be in his shoes when they returned from their day's outing. Lola's little display of temper strengthened Paula's resolve to leave the house as soon as possible.

Once at the rodeo she scanned the crowd anxiously, hoping to see her brother, but without success.

'I'll have to start knocking on doors

tomorrow,' she told Charles, when they were returning to the house at the end of the day. 'I'll try the hotels first, I think, and after that I'll do the rounds of the boarding-houses.'

'Of course, there's something we haven't considered. Bertie may be travelling under an assumed name. After all, he is on the run from an irate father!'

'Joshua Price would never follow him all the way to Canada, would he? No, of course he wouldn't. But if Bertie is calling himself by a different name, I don't know what I'll do to find him!'

A sob escaped her and she allowed herself the comfort of Charles's arms for a long moment.

'Cheer up, old girl,' he told her. 'I won't let you down. We'll set off again first thing tomorrow morning, and if Bertie is anywhere in Calgary, we'll find him.'

But a nasty shock awaited them at the Kings' home. They were greeted at the door by the maid, who smiled brightly at Charles.

'There's a cablegram come for you sir.'

'Drat!' Charles slit open the envelope. 'I hope there's nothing wrong at the office. I'm pretty sure I tied up all the loose ends before I left.'

He glanced at the message and groaned.

'What is it?'

'This is from your mother, Paula. Just listen. *Bertram safely returned home, stop. Paula to return at once, stop. Letter following.*'

Paula sank down on a handy chair.

'What can it mean?'

'I should think that's obvious,' Charles said, his expression grim. 'The boy has never been in Calgary at all. You've been sent on a wild goose chase.'

'But we had a note that was postmarked Calgary. How did he manage that, if he was never here?'

'Don't ask me. We shall have to wait until Aunt Lydia's letter comes and hope that it puts us in the picture.'

'What about me? Oh, this is too bad of Bertie. I'll have to make my way back to England alone instead of making the journey with you and the Kings. You'll be here for weeks yet, and I can't expect them to give me houseroom for all that time. I've already outstayed my welcome.'

'I'm sure that isn't the case at all.'

Men could be so obtuse at times, Paula decided.

A New Job

Reading the newspaper for want of anything better to do, Paula found herself looking at the situations wanted and offered. She was intrigued by one advertisement that sought the services of a third class teacher for a rural school. The location was at something called S.S. number 5, Lyman's Creek. Applicants were asked to approach a Mr Lyman, who would be at the Balmoral Hotel on certain days.

A glance at the calendar showed her that this was the last of those dates.

On impulse she crammed her hat on her head, picked up her handbag and fled from the house. The Balmoral Hotel was not as grand as its name implied. It was one of the many wooden buildings on a side street, not yet weathered by the passing seasons.

'Mr Lyman, please,' she told the

bored receptionist at the front desk.
'Whom shall I say is calling?'
'He won't know me. Please just say I've come for an interview about the job.'
'Very well, miss. Take a seat, please, and I'll see if he's available.'
It appeared that Mr Lyman was. Paula was shown into a pleasantly appointed lounge, and given a cup of tea.
Mr Lyman was a tall man with a weatherbeaten complexion. He looked more like a farmer than anything to do with education.
'How long have you been a school-teacher, Miss Scott?'
Straight to the point. What on earth had possessed her to come here? Still, there was no getting out of it now. She had to speak the truth and shame the devil, as her brother was fond of saying.
'I'm a music teacher, Mr Lyman. Freelance. I go to my pupils' homes to give lessons there.'

'And how long have you been doing that?'

'Ever since I passed my examinations. Almost seven years now.'

'Hm. By the sound of your accent you come from England. I suppose you went to school there?'

Paula bridled.

'Of course I went to school! Most British children do, you know!'

'No need to get uppity, miss! I thought you might have had a governess at home, that's all.'

'Oh. I'm sorry.'

'Look here, the position is this. The teacher we hired back in the spring has run off with a travelling salesman. That leaves us in the lurch, and the children have already lost a week of school. We have to find somebody in a hurry, and if you're prepared to take it on until Christmas, that will be a great help. We might even be able to find a small bonus as an incentive.'

Paula's head whirled. What on earth had she got herself into?

'Er, what kind of school is it? I'm sorry; I don't mean to sound silly. It's just that I've only just arrived in Canada and I don't quite know . . . '

'It's a rural school. A one-room schoolhouse, the likes of which you'll find all over Canada. All eight grades are taught in one room, by one teacher. We only have twenty-seven children at the moment, so you won't find it too hard. The older ones will lend a hand with the younger ones. Textbooks are provided for the teacher but I daresay you won't need them. The three Rs are the same all over the world, I daresay.'

'Where do I stay, Mr Lyman? Is there a schoolhouse attached?' Paula's thoughts went to some of the rural schools she'd seen in England, where accommodation was provided for the head teacher.

'No problem there. You'll board round.'

'Board round?'

'You are a greenhorn, aren't you? It means you stay at your pupils' homes for a month, turn and turn about.'

'Oh.'

Paula wasn't sure how she felt about that. What if she found herself in a house where conditions weren't up to scratch, or she didn't like the people?

Mr Lyman seemed to read her mind.

'Our people are a pretty mixed bunch. If you don't care for one lot, you'd be out of there by the end of the month. That's how it works, do you see?'

Out of the frying-pan into the fire, Paula thought. Mr Lyman stirred in his seat, no doubt becoming impatient. She had to speak up and say quite firmly that she wasn't prepared to take it on. It was madness, in fact.

'Any more questions?'

'Um, I'm not sure, Mr Lyman. This is all new to me.'

'Well, I tell you what: I'll be leaving at ten in the morning. Be here at quarter to if you want the job. Good day to you.'

In a daze, Paula left the Balmoral. To

quote Elsie, what had she 'been and gone and done'?

* * *

'Where have you been, Paula?' Charles looked her up and down, his expression stern. 'I was beginning to get worried.'

'I've got a job!' she announced.

'A job? How? What sort of job?'

'I'm going to be a schoolteacher. At a place called Lyman's Creek.'

'You're going to teach music out on the prairie somewhere? For how long? And how do you propose to get there? And how will you manage if you get lost in the middle of nowhere?'

'It's all arranged, Charles. I'll be travelling with Mr Lyman, the man who hired me.'

Lola tittered.

'How do you know he's not a white slaver, Paula? He may whisk you off into some sheikh's harem!'

'Lola, really!' Her mother, who had entered the room while this was going on, showed her shock and displeasure. 'White slavers, indeed! What does a gently nurtured girl of your age know of such things?'

Lola laughed.

'Oh, Mama, really! I'm not a child! I read about it in the novel I bought the other day. This girl, Emily Lablonde, believes she's going to the Orient to act as governess to a motherless boy, but instead she meets a handsome sheikh, and . . . '

'Quiet, girl! I don't wish to hear about it. And if I find you buying any more of that nonsense your father will stop your allowance. As for what Miss Scott chooses to do with her life, it is none of our business.'

By the look on the woman's face Paula surmised that Mrs King would be only too pleased if Paula were to be carried out of their lives, sheikh or otherwise.

'Ladies, would you mind if I have a word with my cousin in private?' Charles asked. 'And I'd like to speak to

Mr King, if he's available.'

Left alone with Paula, Charles read her a lecture, most of which she ignored. When he finally ran out of steam she took a deep breath and began to speak.

'I'm fed up with everyone arranging my life to suit themselves! First Bertie upsets everyone at home, and then Mother orders me to travel thousands of miles to track him down. I'm like a pawn in a chess game, moved here and there on some giant board. That cable from Mother was the last straw, Charles! The prodigal son has returned, and now I'm to be moved on again. Well, I won't have it! I'm going to do what I want, for a change.'

'Isn't this a bit drastic? And I'm not sure what the legal implications are. Can someone just enter the country and decide to stay? There must be rules and regulations?'

'This job is only until Christmas, Charles. If anyone asks, I can say I'm here on an extended vacation.'

'And what happens after that? By then I'll have returned to England and the Kings will have gone. You'll be all alone here, with no home and no money. No, Paula, it's not on. I simply cannot allow it!'

'Really? How do you propose to stop me? I'll have the money from my salary, and I do have a return ticket for the ship, remember.'

'If it hasn't expired by then!'

'In that case, please cash it in for me, and send the money to Lyman's Creek.'

'What's going on here?' Samuel King had entered the room on slippered feet, unheard by the two combatants.

'It appears that my cousin means to stay in Canada instead of returning home with us,' Charles snapped. 'I've just been telling her that as her only male relative in this country I cannot permit it.'

'I thought her brother was here. Albert, or whatever his name is.'

'Bertram,' Paula supplied. 'It seems

that I've missed him. He's on his way home.'

'I say, that's a bit thick, isn't it? He knew you were coming, so why has he dodged off like that? He's not in any kind of trouble, is he?'

'My mother needed him.'

That was no lie. This whole debacle had come about because Lydia Scott was desperate to have her younger child back under her roof.

'Then surely you are needed at home.'

'It's not as simple as that, Mr King. The fact is, I can't impinge on your kind hospitality any longer, so I've taken on a temporary job as a teacher in a country school. I'm to travel there tomorrow with a Mr Lyman, who has hired me. Cousin Charles seems to think that I'll be in some danger if I go with him.'

Paula went on to explain how she had seen the job advertised in 'The Herald'.

Mr King shrugged.

'Well, it's not what I'd want for our Lola, but it sounds respectable enough. Charles, you go down to the Balmoral with Miss Scott in the morning and give this Lyman chap the once-over. Explain that you're a lawyer, and ask for his references. If he's any kind of a decent fellow he'll appreciate that.'

'I certainly shall! Paula, how are you going to explain this to Aunt Lydia? She won't be best pleased, you know!'

'She has a bit of explaining to do to me,' Paula said, her lip thrust out mutinously. 'Or, at least, Bertie does!'

'She said in her cable that a letter is on the way. No doubt it contains the whole story. You'll miss that, of course, if you insist on leaving in the morning.'

'You can redirect the letter, can't you?'

Trying to hold back tears Paula rushed out of the room, letting the door swing to behind her.

* * *

The school was not what Paula had expected. It was a small, wooden building, standing in the middle of a vast expanse of flat land, which seemed to stretch for ever until it met the horizon.

When Mr Lyman flung open the door she caught her first glimpse of the room where she was meant to be spending her days for the next few months. There were no proper desks, just rows of rough wooden benches, every one of them backless. She pitied the children who would have to sit on them for hours on end.

At one end of the room a lonely chair, of the kitchen variety, perched on a low platform made of unfinished plans.

'That's for you,' Mr Lyman informed her.

'I shall need a table, Mr. Lyman. I cannot mark the children's work with their slates resting on my knee.'

'I'll see what I can do. The last teacher managed perfectly well without one, but, of course, you're from England. You're used to fancier ways. There's a blackboard coming,' he said proudly. 'That'll make all the difference.'

'It will indeed,' Paula agreed. She wondered how the previous teacher had managed.

It occurred to her that there were no houses within sight of the school. They had come here directly after leaving the train, Mr Lyman having collected his horse and buggy from the livery stable at what passed for the hamlet of Lyman's Creek.

'How do the children come to school, Mr Lyman?'

'They walk, most of them, except for one or two that have ponies. That's what a school section is, you see. When setting up a School Board here we take a look at where the settlers are, and then we build on a spot it's possible for all the youngsters to reach. We've done pretty well here. No child has to come more than four miles to attend our school.'

'Four miles each way?' Paula squeaked. She saw herself limping four miles home after a tiring day of teaching.

'Of course, if that's too much for you,' Mr King said, with a look of scorn on his face, 'I daresay I could find a nice driving horse for you. That's if you have the money to pay for it, of course. Our budget doesn't run to things like that.'

'I'm sure I shall manage very well,' she told him.

If those poor little prairie children could manage it — probably barefoot, at that — she certainly wasn't about to be outdone.

A thought struck her.

'And where are the, er, facilities?'

'There's a grand new outhouse, and we've just had a well dug here, so you won't find finer facilities in all the land.'

Mr Lyman beamed proudly and received a weak smile in response.

'Now, then, if you've seen all you came to see, we'd best be on our way.

Mrs McGregor is expecting you.'

'Is that where I'll be staying?' Paula wondered.

'Yes, indeed; for the first month, that is. You'll be moving on to another house in October.'

From the outside the McGregor home looked decent enough, although small. A flourishing kitchen garden off to the side gave promise of some nourishing meals, and Paula's spirits lifted as she surveyed her new, if temporary, home.

The woman who came bustling out to meet her was a middle-aged, smiling body, wrapped in a floral pinafore.

'You'll be Miss Scott, then. Come away in! You've come to the right place, miss, with a name like that! My husband's people came out from Scotland in the Eighties, to settle here. I don't suppose you've any good Scots blood yourself?'

'I'm afraid not,' Paula said, smiling in response.

'Ah, well, I daresay we'll get along

well enough, in spite of that. Will you not come in, Mr Lyman, and take a drop of tea? It's thirsty sort of weather, that it is.'

'Thank you, Mrs McGregor, but I cannot stop. My wife is expecting me. If I don't put in an appearance soon she'll think I've eloped with Miss Scott, here!'

Paula hardly knew what to make of this remark but evidently the two knew each other quite well for her hostess laughed heartily.

'Get along with you, Mr Lyman! Whatever next?'

'I'll show you to your room, Miss Scott,' Mrs McGregor said, when the school trustee had driven away. 'I daresay you'll be wanting a wash after coming all this way, so I'll bring up a jug of hot water by and by. It won't take long; I've a kettle on the stove, just coming up to the boil. And do call me Edith; that's my name. We don't stand on ceremony here.'

'And I'm Paula.'

'Paula! That's an unusual name. Very pretty.'

The room to which Paula was taken was tucked under the eaves at the top of the house. Evidently following the roofline the walls came down to within a foot of the floor.

'You'll need to be careful not to stand up in a hurry when you get up in the morning,' Edith said, 'or you'll get a nasty crack on the head. You'll soon get used to the way of things, though. This is my girls' room. They move out and sleep downstairs when we board the teacher.'

'Oh, dear! I don't want to put them out. Perhaps I could sleep downstairs instead?'

'That you could not! My man gets up at four in the morning to start work. He'd be that mortified to find the teacher stretched out downstairs! Don't you worry about Ruby and Eva! They're used to this and they enjoy being down in the midst of things well after their bedtime. Some day we'll have a guest room, perhaps, but for now we must make do the best we may. Now, Miss Scott, you unpack your things and I'll have a jug of hot water up here in a jiffy.'

Left alone, Paula gazed around her. The room was sparsely furnished, although spotlessly clean. A large bed took up most of the space, the only other item of furniture being a wash-stand holding a jug and basin of heavy rose-patterned china. She peeped under the bed and was relieved to find a large chamber pot that was also festooned with roses. Her discovery of the state of plumbing facilities in this part of the world had come as a shock. Mother would have forty fits if she were to be faced with anything so primitive. Luckily, Mother was far away in civilized Wimbledon.

'I was wondering, Mrs McGregor, where we are?' Paula asked, when that lady returned with towels over her arm and a steaming jug in her hand.

Mrs McGregor looked puzzled.

'This is our farm. What did you want to know, exactly?'

'I mean, what is this place called? Mr Lyman told me I was coming to teach at Lyman's Creek, but there doesn't seem to be any town or village hereabouts. That place where we got off the train seemed to be called Lyman's Halt.'

Mrs McGregor laughed.

'Bless you, child. If we stay here long enough civilisation may come to us, but in the meantime we're all stuck out in Meredith Township. Saul Lyman's grandfather was the first settler here, which is how the creek got its name. We're not so far out in the wilds as you may think. When we go to church on Sunday you'll see a few more houses round about, but nobody in the country has close neighbours. That's the way things work out here.'

'I see. By the way, I'm longing to meet the children. Where are they? Out playing?'

Mrs McGregor looked shocked.

'Oh, no, Miss Scott! They all have

their chores to do. This is a working farm. Every one has to pull his weight if they want to eat. That's why you won't see much of the school section's older boys until the snow flies. They're needed on the farms, you see.'

'But that's dreadful!' Paula stammered. 'Don't their parents want them to have an education?'

Perhaps when she got herself firmly entrenched she should start a campaign against child labour.

Mrs McGregor's face wore an expression that suggested that Paula had a lot to learn.

'The people here are farmers,' she said mildly. 'They must work hard in order to succeed. Perhaps you don't know, Miss Scott, that when the settlers first came here the land hadn't been touched since the Lord made it. Clearing it and making it fit to plant is full-time, back-breaking toil and fortunate are those who have sturdy sons to help in the process.' She shook her head. 'I could tell you stories, Miss

Scott, and maybe I will some winter evening when we're sitting down with our mending baskets on our knees. Why, I've seen women hitched to the plough in place of a horse to help their men folk clear the land. I count myself lucky I've not had to do that, but there, we do what we have to do. Survival is everything in these parts, Miss Scott.'

Hanging her Sunday dress on the row of hooks that served in place of a wardrobe, Paula thought about what she had just heard. She was already learning a great deal about the life of a pioneer family, and she realised that it would be best if she kept quiet and listened to everything that was going on around her. She didn't want to come across as a know-it-all, and she was sure that if she spoke out of turn these hardy pioneer women would curl their lips in scorn.

While on the subject of scorn she thought of Lola King. Paula could well imagine how that young woman would react if set down at Lyman's Creek!

With a pang, she wondered how Charles was getting along. Lola would probably be all sweetness and light now that Paula was out of he picture. Would Charles be besotted by his fiancée now that there was no competition in the house and allow himself to be manipulated by her?

She must stop thinking, Paula told herself, setting her second-best pair of shoes on the floor with a bang. He didn't belong to her and he never would, so she should get used to it!

Easier said than done, of course, but for Charles's sake she hoped that Lola's nicer side would prevail once she was married, and they would make a happy life together.

Meanwhile, Paula was embarking on an exciting adventure, here in pioneer country. If she found her vocation as a schoolteacher, perhaps she would stay on in Canada. Possibly that would not be at Lyman's Creek, but in one of the cities, where she might find the amenities she had been used to.

Prairie School

'Good morning, children. I am Miss Scott.' She looked around. 'Before we begin lessons I want to make up a register,' she told them. 'I shall go around the class and asked each of you in turn to give me your names, and your father's name as well.'

She pointed to Ruby McGregor, who was seated in the first row.

'I'll begin with you, Ruby. Give me your name, please.'

'But you know me, miss! I'm Ruby!'

The class erupted in giggles. The child had spoken in innocent bewilderment, not intending to be rude, but Paula knew that she must not lose control of the pupils.

'Quiet, please! Yes, I know who you are, but as I said, I have to collect the details for the register. If you can answer properly then the other pupils will know what I want them to say. Children whom I don't yet know,' she added. 'And stand up when you speak to me, please.'

The child nodded and scrambled to her feet.

'My name is Ruby McGregor and my daddy is Ross McGregor.'

'That's very good, Ruby. You may sit down.' Paula turned her attention to a boy on the next bench. 'Now, then, tell me your name, and explain who your father is.'

'Sean O'Hare,' he muttered. 'Me da is Paddy O'Hare.'

'You may sit down. Next?'

She waved her pointer at a slightly older boy, who stood up readily enough but said nothing.

'Yes? Your name, please?' Still no response. Was the child deaf?

'Tell me your name,' she repeated, stretching her lips wide with every syllable in case the child could lip read. This time he said something she didn't understand.

Next to him, an older boy put up his hand.

'Please, miss, his name's Stan, and he don't speak no English. He's Polish or something like that. They just come here last week, see. My mam says we gotta make allowances cause he ain't had no chance to learn to talk like a Christian yet.'

'Thank you. All of us will make allowances, won't we? And I believe that Poland is a very Christian country, so perhaps it would be better to say that Stan doesn't speak like a Canadian yet. And your name is?'

Somehow the first part of the morning went by, and Paula sent the children outside for playtime, which was known to them as recess. Whatever it was called, she now understood that it must have been invented as much for the teacher's benefit as for the pupils.

If she managed to get through this day without collapsing, she would be able to tackle anything!

Later on, she resorted to sign

language in order to communicate with Stan. Pointing to herself, she mouthed 'Miss Scott.' Then she wrote her name on the blackboard. Moving to Stan's bench she pointed to him, and then to his slate, making a scribbling motion with her hand. He brightened at once, and set to work. He may well have written his name down, but when he held up the slate to her, flushed with his achievement, she saw that the words were incomprehensible to her. All she could do was nod and smile and move on to the next child.

* * *

'How did your first day go?' Edith McGregor asked, when Paula was seated at the kitchen table nursing a well-deserved cup of tea.

'All right, I think. I didn't set them any homework, this being the first day back after the holidays.'

'No harm done, I'm sure, but just mind you keep their noses to the grindstone in future. You don't want them showing you up when the inspector calls.'

Paula's heart sank.

'When does he come? Do you know?'

'Oh, he likes to surprise you, does our Mr Laidlaw. I suppose it's all for the best, keeping the teachers on their toes. You don't want to worry over-much, though. He's strict enough, but they say he's fair.'

Perhaps it didn't matter a great deal if he did mark Paula down, even though it would be a blow to her pride. As a substitute teacher she'd hardly be here long enough to affect anyone's education.

'As far as I can tell, most of the children seem to be right where they should be, in terms of the standards laid down for each grade,' she said. 'Some of them seem quite bright, in fact. The only one I worry about is a young Polish boy, whose name seems to be Stanley or something like that.'

'Oh, that's young Stanislaus. I know

his mother, Rose. She does have a few words of English, but I expect they speak Polish in the home. I imagine he'll soon pick up the language, through playing with the other boys. Now, then, it's shepherd's pie tonight, and if you'd be kind enough to go down cellar and fetch me up a jar of chow-chow, I'll open that to go with it. Liven it up a bit, that will.'

Chow-chow? The only chow that Paula had ever come across was the four-legged variety, but when she descended the wooden stairs to find shelves crammed with hundreds of bottles of preserved fruits and vegetables she was relieved to find that it was a sort of green chutney.

Seemingly the teacher had as much to learn as the children she'd been hired to teach . . . and that included the English language, Canadian style!

'Ross is going to the Creek to pick up a few things for me,' Edith announced some days later. 'Is there anything he can do for you while he's there?'

By now Paula had been in the area long enough to know that the Creek was the crossroads hamlet close to the railroad station. It contained a general store, which stocked everything from tinned goods to farm implements to bolts of cloth that Mrs McGregor referred to as 'yard goods'. There was also a forge and, surprisingly, a tiny millinery establishment. There were no houses as such; each proprietor lived over the shop.

The general store contained the post office, which was simply a desk and some cupboards behind a grille. Incoming and outgoing mail travelled by train; of course there was no household mail delivery.

'I'd be glad if he'd take a letter for me,' Paula said. 'I've written to my mother and I know she'll be looking forward to receiving a letter from me.'

That might well be the case, Paula knew, but she wouldn't be so happy when she'd read what Paula had to tell her!

It was to be hoped that Elsie had a good supply of Mother's pills to hand for use when the blow fell.

* * *

'There's a letter for you!' Edith said, when Paula and the children arrived home from school. 'Ross picked it up this morning. It's over there, on the what-not.'

'Is there anything to eat, Ma?' one of the boys asked.

'You can have an apple. Then go and get on with your homework.'

'Aw, Ma!'

'None of that! Miss Scott is here to see that you get an education, and so you will, if I have anything to do with it. Scoot right now!'

The boy went upstairs, grumbling.

'Perhaps you'd like to read that letter in privacy,' Edith said. 'I thought it would be from your ma, but the postmark says Calgary. Maybe it's from your young man, eh?'

'I think I will go up and have a wash,' Paula agreed, clutching the bulky envelope. 'It was pretty dusty coming over the trail.'

'Don't I know it! They tell us we'll have proper roads out here in the future. I hope I live to see that day.' She picked up her rolling-pin and began to attack her pastry.

Paula mounted the stairs and entered her bedroom. She'd recognised Charles's handwriting and by the look of things he'd written her a lovely long letter.

When she'd torn open the envelope she was disappointed to find that it contained a letter from England. Lydia had addressed the missive in care of Mrs Samuel King and now Charles had sent it on. Obviously Mother hadn't received anything from Paula when she'd written this, and their letters had crossed in the post.

There was just a short note from Charles.

Hope all is well. I still think you're mad, but you're a free woman. I'm sending on this letter from Aunt Lydia. Must dash. All my love, Charles.

All his love. If only he meant it! Disappointed, Paula opened her mother's letter. She scanned the pages.

I hope that you are having a lovely time in Calgary, and that you will now be ready to return home. You will be glad to know that dear Bertie has returned to the fold. It seems that the silly boy was not in Canada at all. In fact, he never left England. You will remember that note he sent us? Well, the fact is, he gave it to someone else to post, a friend who really was on his way to Calgary.

It was very naughty of him, but he explains that he didn't know what he was doing, being so distressed over the false accusations made by that wicked girl.

As I said, he is back at home now, and there is no need for you to remain abroad. All this worry has quite upset my poor heart, and Elsie has had to visit the doctor to obtain a further supply of my pills. It is a great comfort to me to know that I shall have my daughter at my side for the rest of my days.

Ever your loving mother.

Lydia Scott.

Paula flung down the letter and went to the dormer window, looking out on the peaceful scene. Any day now she would receive another letter, full of recriminations. Well, Mother would just have to swallow her resentment because Paula was contracted to teach here until Christmas. She supposed that she could break that contract if Mother was ill, but she hoped it wouldn't come to that. Apart from not wishing to let the School Board down at this stage, she was quite enjoying the experience of teaching these youngsters.

'Curse you, Bertie Scott!' she muttered. It just wasn't fair! Bertie was the one at fault here, but his exploits had been written off as the doings of a naughty boy. He was a grown man, for goodness' sake; quite old enough to take responsibility for his own actions!

And what about Paula? There was no hint of an apology for all the trouble she had gone to, travelling thousands of miles from home on a wild goose chase! It didn't matter that she had enjoyed every minute of the experience; it was the principle of the thing.

Now, like a puppet on a string, she was about to be jerked back to England.

'No, I'm jolly well not!' she said aloud. 'They can't make me go back. I'm sorry if Mother is upset, of course I am, but let Bertie dance attendance on her for a bit. He's the blue-eyed boy, and I'm just their handmaiden!'

Needless to say, this show of defiance led to an upsurge of guilt, and Paula was wiping a tear from her eye when a knock came at the door.

'Please, miss! I can't do this reading. The words are too hard. Please, can you help me?'

'I'll be there in just a minute, Ruby,' Paula said. 'Go downstairs and wait for me, please.'

She wondered about the ethics of giving what amounted to special coaching to a particular child but soon dismissed the thought. She was to 'board round', and no doubt she would be asked for similar privileges in the other homes in which she stayed. If the subject ever came up she would say that she wanted to give value for money by going the extra mile.

It was only later, when she was setting the table for supper, that a thought struck her. What was happening with the Prices? Mother hadn't said. Surely Bertie couldn't be lounging around at home if there was any danger of the court case being pursued? And with Charles being out of the country, Mother would have had to engage another solicitor — and possibly a barrister as well — to act in Bertie's defence. That would not please her, especially if it meant the whole sordid tale being made public.

'How are things with your young

man?' Edith asked, wielding the potato masher.

'He's not my young man, he's my cousin. And he doesn't say too much. Actually the letter was from my mother. Charles has just sent it on.'

'Lovely. What does she have to say?'

'Not a great deal. Just confirming what she said in the cable, that my brother is at home again. She wants me to return home at once.'

Edith put down her saucepan.

'Well, now, you can't do that, can you? You're promised to us until Christmas, and if all goes well I expect the trustees will offer you the post permanently. Should you like that?'

'Mother would never allow it,' Paula told her.

'Now you listen to me, my girl! Perhaps it isn't my place to say this, and I know we owe a duty to our parents, like the Good Book says, but you don't want to be too quick to jump to her tune. Just you remember poor Maggie Oates!'

'Maggie Oates?'

'Oh, you don't know her yet. Well, Maggie was the only girl in a family of eight children, all the rest being sons. She was a pretty girl when she was young, and the boys were around her like bees at a honey-pot. She was engaged to marry a young farmer from the next section, but her mother took a turn and Maggie agreed to put off the wedding until the old woman was better. Well, each time they set a new date, old Mrs Oates would take another turn, and finally Maggie's chap got tired of waiting and he up and married somebody else.

'The parents got older and older, as people do, and the old man promised Maggie he'd see her right if she stayed on to care for them. She did that, faithful as you please, but did she get help from those brothers of hers, or their wives? She did not! And when the old ones died and the boys inherited the farm, not a penny piece did Maggie get.'

'Where is she now?'

'She's still around. Maid at the Leach farm, working all hours inside and out, that's Maggie. I doubt they can afford to pay her much, and she's getting up in years now, so one of these days she'll drop in her tracks and that'll be the end of poor Maggie Oates. You learn a lesson, Paula Scott, and think twice before you commit yourself to a life of drudgery!'

Paula looked thoughtful. Spending her life with Mother could scarcely be compared with the trials of the unknown Maggie Oates. They had a comfortable home in Wimbledon, with Elsie to do the housework and provide the meals. They might not be rolling in wealth, but there was always enough for the occasional new frock or hat, not to mention the violet-centred chocolate creams that Lydia adored. It was a life many women would envy.

But don't forget Bertie! a little voice said. Mother could not live for ever and Bertie was sure to marry. What would his wife make of a dependant sister-in-law hanging round their necks like an albatross? Would this unknown woman urge the unreliable Bertie to live up to his obligations, or would it be a case of poor Maggie Oates all over again? Paula could end her days in a bedsitter, living on tea and toast and cooking on a gas ring.

Pot Luck

'We're having our fall pot luck on Sunday,' Edith McGregor said cheerfully. 'It will give you a chance to meet the neighbours and I know they'll all be curious to meet you, being fresh out from the Old Country. Don't be surprised if all the women want to know about the latest fashions back there.'

Paula wondered what good it would do these prairie women in their drab, practical garments. The hems of their dresses were frequently stained with mud and their faces under their limp sunbonnets were burned brown with the relentless sun. Perhaps they liked to dream of happier things. Her thoughts went to Lola in her expensive silks and taffetas, whose white hands had never peeled a potato or scrubbed a floor.

'And when we're done, you'll be

moving over to the Foley place,' Edith went on. 'I must say I've enjoyed having you here, Paula.'

'And I've enjoyed being here,' Paula assured her. She had discovered that Canadians referred to autumn as 'fall' — something to do with the leaves falling off the trees, she supposed — but she wasn't sure what a 'pot luck' was.

'Oh, all the women take a dish of something for the meal,' Edith explained. 'Mind you, what you see is what you get, if everyone decides to take the same thing. We could end up with ten bowls of potatoes and not much else! Still, it always seems to work out in the end.'

As Sunday drew closer, Paula's apprehension grew. Meeting new people was no problem; she looked forward to getting to know the parents of her pupils. This was often the key to understanding the youngsters. However, moving to a new home was worrisome. She had been comfortable here at the McGregor farm and she didn't know the Foleys at all. Still, it was only for a month, and then she would move on again.

Sunday came, bringing with it fine weather.

'Thank goodness for that,' Edith said. 'We do need rain in the worst way, but not on our pot luck!'

When they arrived at the little church, Paula understood why. The building was plain and unadorned and scarcely bigger than her schoolhouse. Inside, it consisted of a solitary room with a collection of chairs facing a table at the front. It was her first visit to the church, which was visited by a clergyman who served several charges.

'Some day we'll have pews,' Edith said, 'but these chairs aren't too bad for sitting on, unless Reverend Blair rambles on a bit. They are handy, though, because we can carry them outside for the meal. Oh, look, here come the Foleys. No time to introduce you now, for here's the Reverend right behind them.'

The service went by in a blur. Paula joined in the old familiar hymns, glad to show that she knew the words, for there were no hymnbooks in this poverty-stricken place. Mr Blair's sermon was punctuated by the shuffling of feet, and the aroma of peppermint reached her nostrils as her fellow worshippers sucked a sweet or two. Behind her a child cried out, and was instantly shushed by its mother.

Afterwards, standing outside in the cool autumn air, Paula surveyed the scene, wanting to imprint it on her mind to recall in after years when she was back in England. Rows of buggies were lined up nearby, their horses hitched to a long rail. What would happen to the poor beasts in wintertime, when the snow was thick on the ground? Edith had told her that they often had three feet of snow surrounding their house, but Paula suspected that the older woman was teasing her, for how could the children get to school in conditions like that?

The men were now putting up trestle tables which they had retrieved from a lean-to at the back of the church. The women were spreading snowy white bedsheets over the bare wood and bringing baskets of food from the buggies.

'I'm Paddy Foley and this is me wife, Nancy.'

Paula looked up from her musing to see a tall, rangy Irishman standing before her, smiling.

'How do you do?'

'How are ye?' Nancy Foley nodded. 'You know me boys. This is little Bridget. Too young for school yet.'

Looking solemnly at Paula, little Bridget popped her thumb in her mouth. Her mother pulled it out again.

'Stop that, now! Is it buckteeth you'll be wanting, child? You'll end up like me Auntie Nora, and her without a tooth in her head!'

Paula couldn't see the connection, but she smiled at the child, who hid her face in her mother's skirts.

'And this is Jake Marriott,' Foley said, taking a man by the sleeve. 'You'll know his young lad from the school.'

Once again Paula clasped an outstretched hand, smiling up at the newcomer. She knew that this man's wife had died in childbirth some years earlier, trying to give life to twins who had lived just a few hours. All three were buried in a little cemetery on the hill, their lonely graves marked by small wooden crosses.

As yet the man had not remarried. The more romantic of the married women were fond of saying that his heart was buried up there in the grave with his poor Maria, but that may have been just a fantasy.

Paula began to feel uncomfortable under Marriott's searching gaze. He seemed to be peering into her soul as if assessing her worthiness to educate his son.

'Young Peter is doing very well, Mr Marriott,' she murmured.

'Aye, well, he'd better learn all he can

while he has the chance, Miss Scott, for as soon as he's big enough to drive the plough I'll be taking him away from the school. I need all the help I can get now my sister has gone back East.'

Paula swallowed a sharp retort. It would do no good to engage in an argument with the man, and how did she know what was best for the boy, in any case? These farmers led a harsh life on the prairie, and if young Peter was to inherit his father's acreage in time he had to serve an apprenticeship like all the other youngsters.

Edith had told her what she knew about the Marriotts.

'His sister came out to help with the boy, for he was only two years old when his ma was taken. She stayed on for a couple of years because somebody had to look after the child while his father was working the land. You can't leave a youngster alone in the house, especially in winter when there's a fire on.'

'But she's not there now, this sister?'

'Oh, no. She's gone back to the

Ottawa Valley now that Peter is in school. They say she's been writing to some fellow back there all the time she's been away, and now they're getting wed. Jake will miss her, mind, but you can't blame her for going. She has her own life to live after all. Perhaps he'll think about remarrying now he's on his own.'

Aware that Marriott was still looking her up and down, Paula excused herself and moved towards the tables, asking if she could be of help. She didn't like the feeling that he was assessing her as he might do a horse he meant to buy.

'We're all done here,' Edith told her. 'We'll get started as soon as the Reverend asks the blessing.'

As the dishes were passed in her direction, Paula's eyes gleamed at the array of food that was offered. She doubted that any of these families ate so well on a regular basis, but probably each woman had done her best to outdo the others for this occasion. Casseroles of beef, mounds of mashed potatoes and various vegetable dishes had been kept hot in hay boxes since leaving home, and there was plenty of home-made bread, butter and cheese to go with it. Someone had started a fire nearby on which a pot of water was boiling merrily. Hot, strong tea would soon be available for all.

'Look at all them pies, miss!' One of Paula's students nudged her arm, causing her to drop her fork. Fortunately the potato missed her dress and landed on her plate.

Indeed, the array of desserts on the nearby table was enough to satisfy anyone's sweet tooth, yet not a crumb remained at the meal's end.

All too soon Paula's trunk was transferred to the Foleys' wagon, and she was whisked away to their home, with the Foley boys racing behind on foot. Her first sight of the house was not impressive, but as Edith had told her the Foleys had not been here as long as the McGregors and it took time to get established.

'You'll be sharing with young Bridget,' Nancy Foley told her, showing the way into a room that was not much bigger than a cupboard. It held a single, sagging bed and Paula hoped fervently that the little girl wasn't a restless sleeper.

Downstairs the house consisted of one large room, with a stove for heating and cooking. Benches were ranged alongside a scarred wooden table, and a curtain hanging from the ceiling concealed a large double bed on which a variety of patchwork quilts were piled.

A large black cross was nailed on the opposite wall, and a variety of what Paula thought of as holy pictures, obviously clipped from a magazine, provided the only other decoration in the room. Nancy saw her guest looking open mouthed at these items, and she smiled ruefully.

'Aye, Miss Scott. We're Catholic.'

'But the church . . . it's Presbyterian! I mean, won't you get into trouble with your priest?'

Nancy shrugged.

'Back home, Father Mulcahy would have a spitting fit, right enough, but what are we supposed to do? The nearest Catholic church is seventy miles away. Besides, it's not just the Presbyterians who go to the Creek church. There's Baptists, Methodists, all sorts. There's yourself, too, a member of the English Church.'

The grapevine had obviously been hard at work.

'It's a good thing they all get on well together, then.'

The other woman grimaced.

'Out here, everybody has to get along with the neighbours, miss. It would be a bad lookout if they didn't, for we depend on each other, you see. And there's another thing. Going to church is an outing, you know? We have a bit of a gossip after the service. Get all the news. I couldn't be doing without that.'

Paula nodded. She was beginning to understand the life these prairie women led. Working from dawn until dusk to provide for their families and support their husbands, on these lonely farms with no other human habitation in sight, they must long for a bit of company. Attending the occasional church service, even one that was not of their own faith, must seem like a lifeline thrown to a drowning man.

'We won't need much of a supper after all that food at the church,' Nancy remarked. 'A bit of bread and jam and a cup of tea will do us fine.'

Paula hoped that this wasn't a sign of things to come. Back in England a supper of bread and jam might be something that was served to children of the poorer classes. Still, she chided herself, she mustn't criticise. She was a guest here, and the bread and jam were likely to be homemade. She could do a lot worse.

Later, sitting up in bed with a frightened Bridget stretched out beside her, she reviewed the events of the day.

The young Foley boys had seized the opportunity to tease their teacher.

'You know Peter Marriott, Miss

Scott . . . ' John began.

'Yes, of course. He comes to school, doesn't he?'

'It's his da, see. I think he likes you.' Giggling, James nudged his brother.

'That's a silly thing to say, John,' Paula told him, not quite sure how to handle this.

'Now don't you be bold, John Foley!' his mother said. 'I can see you'll have trouble keeping this pair in order up at the school, Miss Scott. My advice to you is, take a strap to their legs or there'll be no end to their blarney.'

She gave her sons an affectionate look and Paula ignored the fresh outbreak of giggles. There were times when it was best to leave well enough alone.

Canadian Courtship

On Monday morning young Peter Marriott trotted into the school clutching a brown envelope, which he thrust into Paula's hand.

'Thank you, Peter. What is it?'

'It's from my dad.'

'It's a love letter, miss!' John Foley jeered.

Peter reddened and he took a step towards John, with his fists clenched.

'It is not, John Foley! Just shut up!'

'Boys! Boys! Settle down!' Paula ordered. 'It's time for prayers.'

As the assembled children bowed their heads in readiness she heard a whisper from James Foley, directed at Peter Marriott.

'Yer daddy's going courting!'

She decided to ignore this, but she realised that something had to be done, and soon. It seemed that the Foley boys, far from being intimidated by the introduction of the teacher into their home, were encouraged by their close contact with her and feared nothing.

Once she knew what Jake Marriott wanted of her, she could put the boys straight on the walk home after school, issuing a firm reprimand.

It was not until the pupils had gone outside for recess that she had time to look at her letter.

The envelope had once held a communication from a company selling farm tools, and the thrifty Jake had used it again, scrawling her name in thick black letters. The message inside was written more neatly on a sheet of lined paper.

The message was brief and to the point.

Would you do me the honour of allowing me to escort you to the Robinsons' corn boil on the fifteenth? Yours truly, Jacob Marriott.

Well! Was there some truth in what the Foleys had suggested? And what on earth was a corn boil? It sounded like some sort of disease! And who were the Robinsons? She didn't recall meeting them at the church pot luck.

Her first instinct was to refuse the invitation, and then she thought, why not? It was hardly a proposal of marriage, after all, and if the outing didn't go well she didn't have to see him again.

On one hand she didn't want to get her name linked with the handsome widower, but on the other she didn't want to become known as a snob.

In the end she wrote a formal note to Jake, accepting the invitation. She popped it inside Peter's lunch bucket so that he'd be sure to take it home.

'The lads tell me you've had an invitation,' Nancy Foley said slyly. 'You're on to a good thing there, Miss Scott! He's the most eligible fellow in these parts.'

'It's only an invitation to a corn boil, whatever that is.'

'Ah, but I hear the Robinsons are

putting up a platform for dancing, so it should be a good night out. Me and Paddy's invited, too. I'm looking forward to it. I enjoy a jig or two.'

'What will you do with the children?'

'Do? Why, we'll take them with us, of course. Children always come to a do like this. It does them no harm to have a late night now and then.'

'I can travel to the Robinsons' with you, then, can I?'

Nancy Foley looked shocked.

'Oh, no, that wouldn't be the thing at all. Jake will come for you, and see you home after. Now, what are you going to wear, Miss Scott? I suppose I'll have to put on my old gingham, yet again. It can't be helped, for we've no money to buy me a new frock, nor will have, for many a year.'

'What sort of corn do they boil, Mrs Foley? Will they be serving some sort of porridge?'

'Porridge? Why would they want to do that? It's cobs, of course. Served with salt and butter that's a real treat.'

Paula was naturally bewildered. Cobs? Surely that meant what the British called maize, a product fed to livestock. Oh, well, the forthcoming outing would give her something to write about in her letters home.

Speaking of letters home, why had there been no word from Mother? Surely she hadn't cut Paula off because she was furious to learn that her daughter was teaching school to little immigrant children?

But, no, that wasn't Lydia's way. She preferred to chew over a subject until every nuance had been dissected. What Paula had to look forward to was a missive in which every indignant word leapt off the page. But why hadn't she written?

When he arrived to pick her up, Jake Marriott was smartly dressed in his Sunday suit. Not used to the ways of Canadian courtship Paula half expected him to hand her a bouquet of wildflowers, but that didn't happen.

'Are you ready?' he said and that was

the last word he spoke until they arrived at the Robinson farm half an hour later. Paula felt that it was up to her to make conversation, so once or twice she made a comment about the weather, a remark that was greeted with a grunt. Peter, hunched down in the buggy, was equally quiet, although he brightened when he saw his schoolmates in a game of tag.

'Off you go, son!' Jake patted his son on the head and the boy sped away, leaving Paula wondering what to do next. 'Come on. I'll introduce you to the folks.'

Stumbling in his wake over the rough grass, Paula was grateful when they were stopped by a plump older woman who introduced herself as their hostess.

'I'm Betsy Robinson. We didn't get to church on Sunday because my grandson had the croup.'

'I hope he's better now?'

'Oh, yes. It's marvellous what a steaming kettle will do. It's just that my daughter-in-law was so worried. You know what first-time mothers are like! Enough about that! The corn should be ready by now. Do you like corn on the cob? And there's ice-cold raspberry vinegar to drink.'

'I don't think that people eat corn in England.' And that vinegar sounded awful!

'Bless you, child! This is sweetcorn. A real treat at this time of year. Off you go, Jake, and get Miss Scott something to eat before it's all gone.'

The corn was steaming in a huge cauldron. Jake took up a pair or tongs and deftly placed a cob on a plate.

'You eat it in your fingers,' he said, when she looked around for a knife and fork. 'Roll it in that pat of butter there, add a bit of salt and you'll be all set. Mind you don't burn your fingers, though. It's hot!'

Nibbling at the cob, Paula had to agree that it wasn't too bad, although doubtless an acquired taste. The raspberry vinegar, however, was a delicious drink and she was grateful when Jake handed her a second glass.

The sound of fiddlers tuning up drew their attention to the makeshift wooden platform on which the dancing would take place. There were no waltzes or polkas here. Some of the dances seemed familiar — Strip The Willow, the Gay Gordons — but at other times the people just seemed to leap and step in time to the music, whooping and screaming to the tune of the merry jigs produced by the fiddlers. Lydia would have called it vulgar, and goodness knew what Lola King would have said, but to Paula the scene simply showed honest folk enjoying a break from their hardworking lives, and she enjoyed herself.

Jake said little on the way back and Paula sat silently with his little boy curled up against her. The Foleys had not yet arrived home and after thanking her escort for a lovely evening she went into the darkened house.

'You must have come home real early,' Nancy remarked at breakfast the next day. 'It was a good night for driving in the moonlight, too. What did you think of Jake Marriott?'

'He's pleasant enough.'

'Is that all? I hoped you two might make a match of it. The man needs a wife and young Peter needs a mother. I think you'd fit in very well there!'

'No, I'm a town girl. I know nothing about farming.'

'Nor do a lot of them that come out to Canada, but you'll never be younger to learn,' Nancy said. 'John Foley, you take your fingers out of that jam before I fetch you a good one round the ear! Don't ask me what I thought I was doing when I decided to get married and have you lot! Maybe you're right, Miss Scott. You're better off single.'

Monday morning produced a flurry of notes. For one wild moment Paula wondered if some, at least, were invitations to further social activities in the district. But one thing was certain: she wouldn't be hearing from Jake Marriott again.

He must have been put off by her lack of small talk, yet it wasn't entirely her fault. They simply had nothing in common, unless you counted young Peter, and Jake hadn't had much to say for himself either.

The first note, handed in by one of the Johnson boys, stated that thirteen-year-old Marie would not be coming to school because she was needed at home to help with the washing.

The next explained that Levi Potvin was 'sick on account of having over-done it on them cobs'. Paula took this to mean that the child's greed had caught up with him, and serve him right, too!

The third note was from Edith McGregor.

Dear Miss Scott, it began formally, although the pair were on first-name terms. *I must apologise on behalf of my husband, to whom you entrusted your recent letter to your dear mother. He carried it to the store in the pocket of his overcoat and forgot all about it. The oversight was not discovered until he gave me the coat for mending, the collar being partly torn off when his young colt took hold of it in his teeth. Rest assured that the letter is now safely on its way.*

Yours faithfully, Edith McGregor. (Mrs)

That explained why there had been no word of complaint from Mother!

Sternly, Paula faced the class.

'Children! This morning I have received notes from some of your parents. Important messages must always be delivered promptly, whether they are addressed to me, or notes I send to your parents. Now, are there any more that I should receive this morning?'

Little Peter Marriott looked up at her warily.

'There's just this one, miss. I was going to give it to you at recess, like Dad told me.'

'Thank you, Peter.'

Holding out her hand Paula glared at the Foley boys, who, whatever they might have been about to say, seemed to change their minds in a hurry.

The note, which she saved to read until the children were outside, was an invitation to go driving on Sunday.

You might like to see the district while the weather lasts. Once the snow flies we'll be kept in until spring.

Were those silly little boys correct in their surmise that she was being courted? Perhaps she would be wise to nip this in the bud right now.

On the other hand she was a little flattered.

'Well!' Nancy Foley enthused, when she heard that news. 'We'll be having a spring wedding, will we?'

'Nothing of the sort!' Paula said. 'We're just friends.'

'Pull the other leg, Paula Scott. I know better!'

'Anyway, I shan't be here in the spring.'

'How's that, then?'

'I've only been hired until Christmas.'

'Nonsense. From what I've heard the trustees seem quite pleased with you. Very likely they'll offer you the chance of teaching here permanently.

'Mind you,' she went on, 'If you do get married they'll have to advertise for someone else because they won't allow a married woman to teach. Stands to reason, does that. With all the work on a farm a woman has no time for anything much outside the home.'

'I am not getting married!' Paula howled. 'You seem to have us wedded when I've only been out with the man once!'

'You could do worse, though. He's a fine-looking fellow, don't you think?'

'Handsome is as handsome does,' Paula muttered, quoting her late grandmother. 'Yes, I suppose he is good-looking, but surely there's more to marriage than that.'

'Jake Marriott is a good catch. His farm is doing nicely, and he has a good watertight house. He's never looked at another woman since his poor wife died. You'll not go far wrong if you set your cap at him, Paula. Why, if I wasn't married, I might just take an interest in the fellow myself.'

'You'd better not let your Paddy hear you say that,' Paula warned, but Nancy only laughed.

'Paddy well knows the side his bread is buttered, girleen, and that's all I have to say on the matter.'

* * *

Once again Jake said little as they drove around the countryside. Such conversation as there was took place between Paula and Peter, the little boy excitedly telling her about the puppies that their collie, Morag, had just produced.

'Can I bring them to school to show the boys, Miss Scott?'

'I don't think so, Peter. They might get lonely away from their mother.'

'Then I'll bring her, too. Can I, Miss Scott? Can I?'

'I'm sorry, dear. I really don't think I

can let you do that.'

'Aw, miss! Why not! Why can't I?'

'Peter Marriott, you stop that this instant!' Jake turned around to frown at his son. 'You heard what Miss Scott said! Just take no for an answer, will you, or you'll feel the weight of my hand!'

The youngster subsided, his lip trembling. Paula felt sorry for him but she didn't like to interfere between father and son.

'I tell you what,' she whispered. 'Tomorrow, at school, you can draw a picture of the puppies to show the other children. How would that be?'

He brightened at once.

'Can I use the pencil crayons, Miss?'

'If you're a good boy.'

The school had recently acquired a brand-new set of coloured pencils, which the children called pencil crayons. If she'd had her way, every child would have such luxuries, but since providing materials for school was the responsibility of the parents and money was tight, most were lucky to have just the basics.

Fortunately, the slates used by the younger children were provided by the school trustees. By the look of them, some slates had been there since Napoleon's time.

'You seem to have a way with children,' Jake remarked, shaking Paula out of reverie. 'Have you many brothers and sisters?'

'Just one; my brother, Bertram.'

'You must like children, though, if you've gone in for teaching?'

'I like children, yes, but I'm not really a teacher. That is, I've taught music — playing the piano, actually — but not in a school setting. Mr Lyman hired me because there was no-one else.'

'Would you like to keep on doing it, as a career, that is?'

'I suppose I wouldn't mind, but I shan't be here much longer. I'm going back to England, you see, when my term is up. My mother wants me at home.'

'Getting on a bit, is she? In frail health, perhaps?'

'I suppose you could say she suffers from her nerves. She's been like that since my father died and as I'm her only daughter she's inclined to lean on me.'

There could be no reply to this, and Jake lapsed into silence again, slapping the reins to encourage the horse. Paula was amazed by this flow of talk and wondered if she should reciprocate, but something held her back.

When they reached the Foley farm again Jake helped her down from the buggy, favouring her with a lop-sided smile.

'December next week!' he remarked.

'Yes, I suppose it is.'

'You'll be moving on, then. Going to the Maxwell place, I've heard.'

'Yes, I believe that's right.'

'Then I'll come over and take you there, Miss Scott. Give you a hand with your trunk. All right?'

'Er, thank you very much,' Paula murmured.

'Right then, we'll be off. See you soon!'

Paula stood at the side of the trail, watching the buggy as it disappeared in a cloud of dust.

What was all that about? Was it simple curiosity, or possibly something more? It was probably just as well that she was returning to England before long, although Wimbledon would never seem the same after her stay at Lyman's Creek. Somehow the people and their way of life had found their way into her heart, especially the children. She would be sorry to leave them behind. And what awaited her in England? Not a teaching job, she was sure, for who would hire her with her lack of qualifications? Some sort of dame school, possibly, paying a pittance and run by an autocratic headmistress who expected long hours of work in return. Life at home with Mother would be better than that.

Cooking Lessons

Annie Maxwell was a pretty fair-haired woman, the mother of seven-year-old Anna Mae, one of Paula's brighter pupils. While she was cheerful enough on the surface her eyes had a look of deep sadness, the reason for which was the loss of two younger daughters some time before.

'It was when the diphtheria came through here,' she explained to Paula. 'Hardly a household was spared, and we lost Mary Rose and Maggie Jane. Do you know what the hardest thing about that is, Miss Scott?'

'I can't imagine,' Paula said, biting her lip.

'Then I'll tell you. It's not having a single photograph to remember them by. Not one! And now I can hardly recall what they looked like. Isn't that a terrible admission for a mother to make? Brian promised me that some day we'd go to the city and get a family photo taken in one of those studios but we never did it. Something always came up to prevent it.'

'You must be thankful that Anna Mae was spared,' Paula said, feeling inadequate.

'That's what people keep telling me,' Annie sighed, 'Or they tell me I'm young; I can have more children. But that won't bring the girls back. They were such sweet little souls, Miss Scott. Now they're buried up there on the hill. At least it's close enough for me to visit their graves, which I can't do with my own family.'

'Are your people all back in England?' Paula wondered.

'Oh, no. My mother is back in Ontario; that's where I'm from. My grandfather came out almost a hundred years ago, so we're well established there.'

'Yet you came out to the prairies!'

'Yes. Brian is one of twelve children,

you see, and there's no way the family farm could support all of them once they were grown up with their own families. Most of them had to move out and make their own way, so when we heard about the land being opened up here we decided to take a chance on it.'

'I see. That was brave of you.'

'A man does what he has to do, and his wife has to follow. That's the way of it, Miss Scott. And what brought you to Canada?'

'I came here to find my brother,' Paula told her, following up with an edited version of Bertie's tale of woe.

Annie's mouth dropped open in surprise as the story unfolded.

'I should have thought it was the other way round! You know, a young woman goes missing, and her brother sets out to find her. I can't imagine travelling thousands of miles on my own to search for any brother of mine. Of course, I've come out here, but I was with Brian.'

'I wasn't alone. I travelled with my

cousin, who happened to be coming to Calgary, where his fiancée's family is staying. Mother would never have let me come, otherwise.'

By the time that Paula had been with the Maxwells for a week, she and Annie had become firm friends. Thus, when the news came, she felt able to let her guard down and explain more about Bertie's entanglement with Mildred Price.

One Saturday morning Brian Maxwell had been to the store to purchase supplies and he returned, beaming, with two letters in his fist.

'One for you, dear — from your ma, by the looks of it — and one for you, Miss Scott.'

Paula accepted the envelope gingerly, expecting it to contain the long-awaited reprimand from Lydia, but to her surprise the letter was from Bertie.

'Of all the nerve!' she spluttered, when she had skimmed through the contents. 'If I could get hold of that little worm right now I'd wring his neck!'

Annie looked up from her own reading.

'What is it, Paula? It's not bad news, I hope.'

Paula crumpled the letter and thrust it into her skirt pocket.

'I suppose it's good news, in a way, but I'm so cross I could scream!'

'Go upstairs and play with your dolly,' Annie said, making a shooing motion towards her daughter.

'But I want to hear Miss Scott scream!'

'Miss Scott isn't going to scream, Anna Mae. It's just something that grown-ups say. Now, run along, and stay up there until I call you down. If you're a good girl we'll make a pan of taffy later, all right?'

The child went off happily enough, and Annie turned her attention to Paula.

'Now, then, are you going to tell me what all this is about, before I die of curiosity?'

Paula pulled the letter out of her

pocket and smoothed it out.

'Here, read it for yourself. I'm just too cross to talk about it!'

Dear Sis, Bertie had written. *The mater seems to think I owe you some sort of explanation, although I can't see how it's my fault that you went haring off to Canada like that. If you'd stayed home and minded your own business you wouldn't be in this pickle now, as the mater puts it.*

Well, you know what happened with La Belle Price and obviously I had to do something about that situation. I did not — I repeat not! — run away to avoid her old man. I went underground while I investigated the whole rotten business. A chum of mine from Oxford days has set up as a private detective and I went to stay with him. He owed me a favour or two, so he agreed to help me out.

The upshot is this. Mildred Price is a married woman and has been for some time. One assumes that the husband is the father of her brat. It turns out that her father didn't approve of him — his name is Cyril Judd — and they were married in secret. Don't ask me why she was still living at home, but that is another story.

I met the girl at a party and we got talking. I suppose I did let drop a word or two about my expectations, but a chap has to say something to impress a girl. She and Judd then decided to set me up, and you know what happened next. The mater feels that old Price was just an innocent bystander. They needed him to come the outraged papa to help make their plan work.

In the end I found out where this Judd was lodging, and I went round and warned him off, with a bop on the snout to emphasize the fact. Luckily I did a bit of boxing when I was up at Oxford so I had him on the ropes before he could say boo. He knows now that if he tries it on again I'll go to the police with the story, so he didn't put up much of a fight.

The mater is furious, of course. She's

all for my going to the peelers regardless, but I think I've managed to persuade her that it could mean the sort of publicity we were trying to avoid in the first place.

So that leaves you, Paula. You may as well come home now. The mater is moaning about all the money wasted in sending you to Canada, but thanks to me you've been able to see the world, which is more than you say for your impoverished brother.

There's one good thing, though. Old Simpson — that's the detective chap — has offered me a partnership in his business, and if I can raise the necessary I may take him up on it. It will be more interesting than any of those boring clerking jobs I've had so far, although the mater is bleating on about it being no job for a gentleman.

Your ever loving brother, Bertie Scott.

'He sounds like a bit of a character,' Annie said, when she had read through this screed.

'Oh, yes, he's a character all right, but a maddening one. You may notice that he expresses not one word of remorse for all this.'

'But does he have anything to be remorseful about? He may have said too much about his future expectations, but that's hardly a crime, is it? He was set up by those Judd people.'

'This is Bertie all over. He sails through life as blithe as you please, giving up jobs because they're boring, getting into muddles, and expecting other people to pick up the pieces. He has no sense of responsibility, Annie. And do you notice how there's nothing about me in all this? He doesn't ask if I'm all right. He doesn't wonder how I feel, having to put my life on hold for his benefit. And who knows what I'll find when I go back to Wimbledon. I shan't have any pupils left at all.'

'He's right in one way, though. Teaching school on the prairie may not be everyone's idea of heaven, but it's been an experience, hasn't it? And unlike most, you can go home when it's over. Most of the women you've met are stuck here, whether they like it or not.'

* * *

'Can you cook?' Jake fired the question at Paula without taking his eyes off the road ahead.

'Cook?' She was taken aback by the question. 'Not exactly.' She frequently heated the hot milk for Mother at bedtime, when Elsie had retired to her room, worn out after her long day. On winter afternoons she sometimes prepared teacakes at the fireside, using a long toasting fork, and if pushed to it she could make a sandwich. As for a proper meal, though, that was a mystery to her.

'What do you mean, not exactly? Hasn't your mother taught you how to cook?'

'Oh, Mother doesn't cook. Elsie sees to all that.'

'Elsie?'

'Our maid. A cook-general, that's her official title.'

'Then how does your mother expect you to cope when you have a husband and children to feed?'

Paula had never considered the fact. All middle-class people in England had at least one servant. If she ever married she would expect her husband to provide her with the necessary staff, according to their position in life.

'I don't know, I suppose most women learn on the job, so to speak. When I was little I sat in the kitchen with Elsie a great deal of the time, when Mother was out paying calls. I probably picked up a great deal by watching her doing the cooking, and failing that, one can always consult a recipe book, I suppose.'

Jake grunted.

'A woman needs to know a deal more than that out here on the prairie. She must know how to bottle fruit and meat. Make jam. Bake cakes and pies and the daily bread. There are none of your fancy shops out here where a woman can go in and buy what she needs, even supposing she had the money.'

'I expect you're right,' Paula murmured. She wondered where on earth this conversation was leading. It almost sounded as if he was interviewing her for the position of wife number two!

'Annie Maxwell is a pretty good cook,' he went on.

'Yes. Yes, she is.'

'Then why not ask her to give you lessons? I'm sure she'd be glad to help.'

'It's something to think about,' Paula replied, thinking it best to give a mild reply. She had enough to worry about without that, for her evenings were spent in lesson preparation. No matter what anyone said, it wasn't easy, teaching pupils in eight different grades simultaneously. In theory the older children helped the little ones, but the difficulty was in making sure they were not short-changed. Added to that there were always undercurrents of mischief in the room as the older boys tended to get up to pranks when her back was turned.

The subject of cooking came up again when the two women were sitting down with their sewing that evening. Paula was putting up the hem of her dress where she had managed to put her foot through it, and Annie was putting together patches for a quilt, using materials that had been culled from worn-out garments. Each block was made up of various strips of colour, with a red square in the middle.

'Something on your mind, Paula? Has Jake upset you in some way?'

'Only that he wants you to give me cooking lessons!'

'What? Well, if that isn't like a man all over. Always thinking of their stomachs.' She stopped speaking suddenly, her needle poised above the cloth. 'Why, Paula Scott, I do believe the man is working up to a proposal of marriage!'

'That's what I'm afraid of. And I just don't know how I'll handle it when it happens.'

'Nonsense! My advice is, snap him up before someone else does!'

'But I don't know if I want him. I'm not in love with him, Annie. And I'm equally sure he's not in love with me.'

'There are other things in a marriage besides a grand passion, Paula. Mutual respect, and for the woman, security, children, all of that. As far as I'm concerned those are the things that will endure. I'm not sure if all that romantic stuff has ever existed outside of the penny novelettes.'

'Did you not feel anything special for Brian, then?'

'Oh, I fancied him, right enough, but I listened to my mum when she told me to look into the future to see if I thought Brian was steady enough for the long haul. Married life was like driving a buggy, she said. You had to put the right horses in the shafts and be careful how you went, so the buggy didn't tip over.'

Paula laughed, but there was some truth in what her friend had said. Not all men could be counted on to maintain a steady course. Bertie was a prime example of that! As far as she could tell, Jake Marriott seemed like a good bet; everyone spoke well of him and seemed willing to push them together.

There was just one thing wrong. Could the pair of them go into marriage heart-whole? Judging by the way that Jake spoke of his first wife, he was still in love with her. Could a new bride compete with that? Could a man love two women at the same time? And what if he could not, and all he wanted was a glorified housekeeper and someone to help bring up his little boy?

Then there was Paula herself. She knew now that she was deeply in love with Charles Ingram, but he was lost to her as surely as Jake's young wife was to him. Paula knew that she had to go forward unless she was prepared to spend the rest of her life alone, but was it right to enter upon marriage as a sort of business arrangement? Was it even sensible? The world was full of men. Mr Right could be waiting just around the corner. Oh, why did life have to be so difficult?

The following week Paula presented Jake with a cake she'd made herself, under Annie's direction.

'Spice cake,' she said proudly.

'Not bad,' he mumbled, through a shower of crumbs. 'Next time, try chocolate. That's the boy's favourite; mine, too.'

'With lots of frosting!' Peter said. 'And will you make me a birthday cake, Miss Scott? With candles on?'

'You'll have to wait a while for that, boy,' Jake said. 'Your birthday's not until April.'

'Aw, Dad!'

'I'm afraid I shan't be here in April,' Paula told the child. 'Perhaps I can make you something special before I leave.'

'Where are you going, miss? Why can't you stay here with us?'

'I've just been hired for this one term, Peter. I'm filling in until they can find a proper teacher.'

'But you are a proper teacher, miss! You teach us arithmetic and all that stuff. I want you to stay until I get as tall as my bedroom door!'

Paula was bewildered.

'Why should you want to get as tall as your door, Peter? I don't understand.'

'You know, miss! Every birthday Dad takes a yardstick and he measures me, and puts a mark on the doorframe, to show how much I've grown. See?'

Paula was suddenly overcome by a bittersweet memory of her own father doing something similar. She wiped away a tear, aware that Jake was looking at her curiously.

'Is there something wrong?'

'No.' She sighed, reaching for the hankie in her jacket pocket. 'I was just remembering my own father. He used to do that, too. He died when I was only thirteen. It was a massive heart attack, the doctor told us. Bertie had just turned nine. I sometimes think it's the reason he's turned out to be a bit shiftless. Mother probably doted on him a bit too much and he's grown up thinking the world owes him a living, especially since he's due to inherit money some day.'

'Aye, a boy needs a man to look up to. Of course, he needs a mother, too, to teach him his manners and such.'

Sensing danger, Paula quickly changed the subject.

'Annie says she'll show me how to make pastry the next time. Her husband is very partial to a fruit pie and they have a lot of apples put by in the loft. Actually, she was wondering if you two would like to come for supper on Saturday. She means to make chicken stew with dumplings, and if my pie turns out well, she'll serve that for dessert.'

'Tell Mrs Maxwell thank you, we'll be there. I want a word with Brian in any case. From what I've heard tell the parents are right pleased with all you've been doing, and it seems to me we should talk to the trustees about keeping you on for the rest of the year.'

'Well, I'm flattered, but . . . '

'Don't thank me yet. But I don't see why they should refuse, unless one of them has the name of a young niece or cousin he plans to put forward.'

What was the point of arguing? As he said, she hadn't been offered the job yet. If and when that happened, she could pleasantly refuse, and that would be that. Or perhaps . . . She closed her mind on the thought.

A Visitor

Lydia's letter was written in the exquisite copperplate handwriting she'd learned in her ladies' seminary in the latter years of Queen Victoria's reign. However, the indentations on the reverse of her monogrammed writing paper showed Paula that Mother had been in some distress when she had penned her letter.

I cannot tell you how I felt when I read your letter. I had received it with joy, hoping to read that you were already on your way home, but how quickly I was disabused of the notion!

The formality of the wording underlined her annoyance, causing Paula to clench her fist as she read on.

To think that a daughter of mine has found it necessary to earn her living in such circumstances is nothing short of a disgrace. While it is always a charitable thing to go among the poor to do what one can to alleviate their suffering, a lady does not accept money for such work. I believe I have been remiss in permitting you to go out and about giving music lessons as I did; I did so only because I felt it right that you should indulge in a little hobby prior to marriage. Now you have brought disgrace on our family by going to the middle of nowhere in this fashion and taking a job! Bertie's fall from grace pales by comparison.

With a rude exclamation Paula crumpled the letter and flung it across the room. Mother was living in the past. There was so much to admire out here on the prairie. The hardworking men, the courageous wives who supported them, the young boys and girls who often walked miles to school, so keen were their parents to achieve an education for their children. They were here to build a brave new world which their grandchildren would some day inherit. How dare Mother refer to them as 'the poor' as if they were layabouts and guttersnipes?

Later, when she had calmed down, Paula tried to see the situation from Lydia's point of view. Her mother had been brought up to believe that ladies and gentlemen did not work for a living. Their gently reared daughters stayed at home under their mothers' protection until they married, whereupon husbands would assume the role of guide and protector.

'You look a bit frazzled,' Annie said, coming inside carrying a basket full of clean laundry. 'You haven't had bad news, I hope? Is your mother all right?'

'She's well enough, if you don't count a temper tantrum as ill health,' Paula muttered, getting up to help fold the sweet-smelling sheets.

'Ah. She's found out what you've been up to, then. Mothers are all the same. Mine nearly had forty fits when we told her we were coming West, and I was a married woman at the time. In her case she was upset because she thought she'd miss seeing the grandchildren growing up. She'd been a pioneer farm child herself, so it wasn't so much the fact that we were having to start from scratch here, clearing the land and all that.'

'Mother just hasn't realised that the world is changing, Annie. You know, for a long time I shared her views about the suffragettes, thinking it unwomanly for them to chain themselves to railings and go about demanding the vote. Now I see that life could hold so much more for us than walking a narrow prescribed route, like a dray horse wearing blinkers. I can't bear the thought of going back to my old life in Wimbledon.'

Annie grinned.

'You know the answer to that one, Paula Scott! Marry Jake Marriott and stay here with your new friends.'

Paula grinned in response.

'I'll give it my earnest consideration.'

The smile stayed on her face as she thought of Lydia's reaction if she received an invitation to a prairie wedding! She would not be able to attend, of course, but she would have plenty to say about it. What if Paula married Jake and told her mother about it afterwards? No, that would be too cruel.

One way or another Lydia would make the best of it, in time. There would be a notice in 'The Times', couched in the usual terms.

At Lyman's Creek, Alberta, Canada . . .

Then there would be the carefully worded announcements to acquaintances, painting the marriage in glowing colours. Jake would become a Canadian landowner; his house would be a sizeable property, standing in its own grounds. None of it would be a lie, exactly; after all the six-hundred-and-forty acres which constituted a farm in Western Canada would sound like a lot to the residents of Wimbledon with their small gardens.

* * *

Paula awoke one morning to find her bedroom in darkness. Fumbling her way to the window she was aghast to see the world engulfed in whirling snow. A blizzard seemed to be raging outside and it was a school day. Breaking the ice in her water jug she hastily washed her face and hands, gasping as the cold water met her skin. Buttoning up her blouse as she went she hastened down to the kitchen, where a blanket of warmth enveloped her.

Annie greeted her cheerfully.

'Hello, Paula! Did you see what's going on outside? You could have stayed in bed for a while, for there'll be no school today.'

'How do you know?'

'Because there never is when the weather's this bad.'

'But I'll have to go to the school, won't I? What if some child turns up and there's nobody there?'

'Well, they won't. The thing about a blizzard is that a person can go in circles, and end up completely lost.

Many a person has perished that way, and we all know it. No parent would let his child go out in this. Why, they'd have trouble just finding their way to the privy and back!'

Sitting at the bare wooden table spooning up oatmeal, Paula was happily aware of the warmth welling up inside her. An unexpected day off; a whole day to herself. What a gift! She would sit near the stove and get on with her knitting.

When she had first arrived at Lyman's Creek Edith McGregor had provided her with some wool and knitting needles. Sighing over the state of her husband's old pullover, the elbows of which consisted of darns upon darns, Edith pronounced that it had outlived its usefulness.

'We'll unravel it, Paula, and after it's had a wash we'll wind it up and use the wool for something else. Do you knit? You can have it, if you like.'

Knitting was one thing that Paula was good at. Elsie had taught her the art when she was very young, and many happy winter evenings had been spent in making socks for charity.

'I've a pattern for mittens if you'd like to use that. You might make some as gifts for the children. We always have a Christmas programme at the school, with a tree, and the teacher usually gives some little gift to each child. I just thought I'd mention it, in case you didn't know.'

'I'm glad you told me. But I don't suppose the youngsters would thank me for giving them mittens. I know that my brother always turned up his nose when he was given something to wear instead of toys!'

'If the children don't, then the parents certainly will. And believe you me, those little ones will be glad to have warm mittens when they're walking to school in January and February. Frost-bite is no joke!'

Edith went through her storage trunk, unearthing small balls of yarn left over from other projects. Now, in

December, Paula had a steadily growing pile of mittens, in all the colours of the rainbow. Building on the dark grey of the original pullover, she knitted striped mittens for each of the boys, and for the girls she embroidered flowers and stars on a plain background. No two pairs were identical. That was deliberate on her part, so there could be no squabbling over ownership.

Now, sitting in the warmth of Annie Maxwell's kitchen, Paula pulled out her mother's letter again. In her dismay she had not read it all the way to the end, and now she felt calmer she felt able to deal with it again. She found that Lydia had a fresh cause for complaint.

Of course, I blame Cousin Charles for this. I allowed you to go to Canada with him on the strict understanding that he would keep you safe. I can't imagine what possessed him to permit you to go into the blue without him. I can only think that he is so wrapped up in his fiancée and their marriage preparations that he has forgotten his obligation to you, and to me! I am seriously displeased and have written to tell him so.

The letter rambled on and Paula put it down again. Poor Charles had certainly done his best; it was Paula who had been wilful. Still, he was man enough to withstand the onslaught of Mother's ire. For a woman who always observed the proprieties to the strictest extent Lydia was being remarkably blinkered. What had been the alternative to Paula's coming to the prairie? How could the Kings have been expected to extend unlimited hospitality to an unwanted guest? It would have taken someone with a thick skin to stay on under those circumstances.

When the weather settled down again Paula found that the journey to school took twice as long as it had before. Trudging through unbroken snow was hard, and having wet skirts flapping round her ankles was a hindrance. Buggies had been put away for the winter and cutters, a type of horse-drawn passenger sleigh, were in use instead. Sometimes a passing farmer would stop to give her a ride, and such courtesies were greatly appreciated. There was something to be said for knowing everyone in the district. Paula could just imagine what Lydia would have said if her daughter had accepted a lift from a passing stranger in Wimbledon.

One blessing here was that a farmer who lived near the school arrived early in the morning to light the stove, so that the building was pleasantly warm when Paula opened up. How she would have managed to light it herself, with half-frozen hands, she didn't dare to think. As it was, the classroom was redolent with the scent of wet wool as the children's garments steamed in the warmth.

Preparations for the Christmas programme were in full swing. Paula asked Annie what was expected of her.

'Well, you'll have carols, of course.

Most of the children know those already, but if you happen to know of one that's new to us, so much the better. Recitations and monologues are popular, and of course the parents will only have eyes for their own children, so each one should have a chance to shine!'

'I wish we had a piano to provide some accompaniment. I wonder if I could borrow Mr Hastings's tuning fork?'

The man in question was an elder at the church, and used the instrument to make sure that the entire congregation began singing at the same pitch.

'Brian has a spare set of sleigh bells.' Annie reached up to a high shelf and handed Paula a strip of leather containing several small bells. 'They jingle nicely, and sleigh bells always remind me of Christmas. Just the thing for the littlest ones to shake in time to the music.'

'Can I do it, Ma?' Anna Mae begged, her eyes gleaming.

'That's for Miss Scott to say.'

The child pouted.

'Oh, I think we can let Anna Mae play the bells,' Paula said. 'After all, they belong to her father. But I'm worried about refreshments, Annie. And how can we possibly serve tea? There isn't a cup in the place.'

'We've got that down to a fine art,' Annie said. 'Each mother makes a loaf of sandwiches and some treats. We borrow a tea urn from the church, and we all bring our own cups. The trustees provide a tree, and each family brings a little gift to put on it for each of their own children. That way nobody gets left out. It also gives people the chance to exchange gifts with friends if they've a mind to. Everything will be well organised without you having to lift a finger.'

That might well be, Paula thought, but there was still plenty for her to do. There were poems and monologues to find — or for her to write if she couldn't find anything suitable. Carols had to be practiced and a welcoming speech prepared. The children spent happy hours in a welter of crayons and paper and flour and water paste, making cards for their parents. This activity was somewhat handicapped by there being only one pair of scissors available, but such was the happy anticipation of the season that nobody seemed to mind.

All in all she was quite pleased with herself, and she was able to turn her attention to helping Annie with the Christmas baking.

On the Saturday before the concert she was doing that when her world was abruptly shaken.

'Miss Scott! Miss Scott! Can you come?' Little Anna Mae had been out in the barn with her father but now came running in, full of excitement. Annie clicked her tongue.

'Anna Mae Maxwell! You're tracking up my clean floor! Haven't I told you to take your boots off before you come into my kitchen?'

'But Dad said he wants Miss Scott. There's a man come to see her.'

'It must be Jake,' Paula murmured, taking her shawl down from its peg. 'Why hasn't he come to the door himself? He knows where to find it.'

The little girl had no answer to that, so Paula stepped outside, gasping in the frosty air, stopping suddenly so that Annie, who had followed her out, stepped on her heel. They both stared at the tall stranger who was now crossing the yard in Brian's wake.

'Sorry, Paula! Who in the world is that?'

'That,' Paula told her, exhaling loudly, 'is my cousin Charles.'

* * *

'Come along, Anna Mae; let's go upstairs and I'll read you a story.'

Introductions had been made, Brian had returned to his chores and now Annie was diplomatically giving Paula and Charles some time alone.

Paula took a deep breath, hoping to quiet her fluttering heart.

'What on earth are you doing here, Charles Ingram?'

'Is that any way to greet your beloved cousin, Paula Scott? You might at least let me get my coat off before interrogating me! You won't believe the trouble I've had finding you. Luckily some chap came along and offered me a lift, or I might still be floundering in the snow bank back there.'

'I'm sorry, Charles. This is such a shock, that's all.'

'A pleasant one, I hope.'

'Of course. Look, would you like a cup of coffee? There's some on the stove, just made a while ago.'

'I certainly would. I'm just about perished with the cold. I've heard that the temperature can fall to minus forty degrees out here, but that sort of thing has to be experienced to be believed.'

Paula smiled as she watched his face when he took his first swallow of the bitter brew. Brian Maxwell always added eggshells to the coffee pot in an attempt to settle the grounds, but even so it took some getting used to. She waited impatiently until he had finished his drink and was able to speak.

'Well, let's have it! What's this all about, Charles?'

'In a word, Lydia!'

'Oh, dear!'

'Yes, oh, dear. I've had a rather strong letter — that's the only way to describe it — from your mother. She's taken me to task for allowing you to come out here, as she puts it, although as I recall I did try to prevent you and you wouldn't listen to me.'

'So what does she expect you to do?'

'I'm supposed to scoop you up and take you back to Calgary with me.'

'I'm sorry, that's just not possible. I've signed a contract that keeps me here until the end of the month. You're a solicitor, Charles. You must know about contracts.'

'Of course I know about contracts,' he said testily. 'But just what did you have in mind to do after that?'

Paula shrugged.

'I might go home, of course.'

'And just how do you expect to do that? Fly like a homing pigeon? I suppose you know that the last voyage to Europe has already left Quebec? Crossings won't begin again until April, or late March at the earliest.'

'Oh.'

'You hadn't thought of that, had you? So I suggest you speak to the school governors and ask them to release you from your contract, which has only a short while to run. You'll return with me to Calgary today and I shall see you settled in some respectable boarding house until you're able to travel back to England.'

But when Paula thought of the children, and how much they were all looking forward to the Christmas concert, she knew that she couldn't let them down. Then, too, the event was a bright spot in the dull lives of their parents and other local residents. How could she just walk away and leave them without a teacher? That would be too cruel. She shook her head.

'I'm sorry that you've come all this way for nothing, Charles, but you'll have to return to Calgary on your own. I've obligations here and I intend to fulfil them.'

'I see. And what happens when January comes and you've no place to go? I suppose you'll expect me to come running to pick up the pieces then? Don't count on that, Paula. I'm already in Lola's bad books by coming here at all. I really don't care to upset her a second time.'

Unkind thoughts of his fiancée welled up in Paula. The woman would have Charles for the rest of her life, if she was lucky. Could she not be gracious enough to spare him for a day or two to help somebody else? Without stopping to think any further she blurted out the first excuse that came into her head.

'Oh, you don't need to worry about

me, Charles Ingram. I'm probably getting married.'

'What!'

'Married, Charles.'

'To whom? Who is this man? Where did you meet him?'

'His name is Jake Marriott. He's a widower, with a young son. Peter is one of my pupils.'

'And what does he do, this widower?'

'He's a successful farmer. He lives about three miles from here.'

'You, a farmer's wife? You're a town girl, born and bred. I can't see you feeding the chickens. And can he afford servants? I can't see you getting your hands dirty, Paula Scott.'

Far from wilting under his scorn, Paula jumped to her feet in a fury.

'How do you know what I can or cannot do, Charles Ingram? Did I say a word to you when you engaged yourself to that spoiled miss back in Calgary? I'm twenty-five years old, this is my life and I shall do as I please, and there's nothing you can do about it. So put that in your pipe and smoke it!'

'You'll live to regret it!' he warned.

'Go away, Charles and leave me alone. Here's your hat and here's your coat. Just go, will you?'

Glowering, he thrust his arms into the sleeves of his coat, and rammed his hat over his ears before marching out of the door.

Annie came running down the stairs, looking concerned.

'Are you going to let him get away like that? I wasn't eavesdropping but I could hear everything through the stovepipe hole. You love him, don't you? Quick! Run after him and let him know. You may never get another chance!'

Looking at her friend for a long moment Paula took up her shawl again and ran to the door, but by the time she reached the verandah Charles had disappeared into the gathering gloom. The thought of him trudging through the snow to reach the railroad station was almost too much to bear. Losing her temper had caused her to say all the wrong things, and now it was too late to call them back. She had lost him. She lowered her head and began to sob.

In view of the fact that she could not travel back to England before spring, Paula decided to ask the school trustees if she might stay on for the rest of the school year. She was well established now, and knew that she enjoyed teaching and she had to live somewhere in the meantime. The Atlantic should be calm in June, making for a pleasant voyage, and by then she would have saved a respectable amount of money, meagre though her salary was. Meanwhile, there was the school concert to look forward to.

Their little community had never heard of fancy wrapping-paper or gift boxes, and she was at a loss as to how to wrap her gifts for the children.

'There's always newspaper,' Annie suggested, but Paula wrinkled her nose at the very idea. Outdated newspapers, cut into squares and neatly threaded on a string, held pride of place in the privies of the district and the thought of presenting her lovingly-made mittens in newsprint repelled her. In the end she decided to hang them on the Christmas tree, providing a splash of colour in the classroom.

On the night of the concert everything went swimmingly. The children performed faultlessly, and as Paula looked around the room she was touched to see the faces of their parents, beaming in the lamplight. Her heart swelled with happiness. Then the blow fell.

Mr Lyman, as head of the board of trustees, lumbered to his feet.

'Before we distribute the gifts I should like to say a few words,' he announced.

'Let's hope he sticks to a few words,' Paula heard one mother say. 'The water's almost boiling and we want our cup of tea!'

'I am sure we are all grateful to Miss Scott for what we have seen here tonight, and for her services over the past few months. For a while there, we thought we should be without a teacher for this term, until our lovely English rose came to the rescue.'

Murmurs of appreciation were heard and someone started to clap. Paula blushed and looked down at her hands, neatly folded in her lap.

'You will be pleased to know that we have secured the services of a new teacher, beginning in January. Miss Clara Rowe of Edmonton will be joining us for the new term. I'm sure that you will all show her a real Lyman's Creek welcome.'

'Are you all right, Paula?' Annie whispered when they were lining up to fill their plates with sandwiches and cake. 'The miserable old buzzard, springing it on you like that! He might have told you earlier.'

Paula gave her a wan smile.

'It's my own fault, I suppose. I should have contacted him earlier. I meant to have a word with him this evening. I had no idea that he would have made other arrangements without speaking to me first. And he did say quite clearly that my engagement was just for one term.'

'And we all know why!' Annie said. 'Clara Rowe is his niece. Her mother was a Lyman, you know.'

Paula attempted to put a brave face on things, smiling and nodding as the parents congratulated her on the success of the concert, wishing her well in her future endeavours. Thus she was only mildly disconcerted when Jake Marriott came up to her and asked if it would be convenient to call on her on Saturday, as he had something to say to her.

Seeing this, Annie gave her the thumbs-up sign. Paula knew that she had some serious thinking to do before Saturday came.

'I've been thinking,' Jake said, shuffling his feet. 'How would it be if we were to get married?'

'To each other?' Paula murmured, wanting there to be no misunderstandings.

'What? Oh, of course to each other. You and me. I believe we'd suit each other well enough, and the boy needs a mother. What do you say, Paula?'

'I'm sorry, Jake. I do like you, and I've become very fond of Peter, but I'm not in love with you.'

'Love? I've tried that, and I came to grief. My dear wife is dead and nothing will bring her back. I never thought of taking on somebody new, but I reckon I'm ready now. You say yes, Paula, and I'll be a good husband to you. I swear I'd never play you false, or treat you meanly unless you deserved it.'

She didn't like the sound of that, but it hardly mattered because she was determined to turn him down, for quite different reasons.

'I'm so sorry, Jake, I really am, but I couldn't marry without love. It wouldn't feel right.' Looking at his crestfallen face and wishing to soften the blow, she went on: 'Besides, my mother is getting on in years. She expects me to return to England to live with her.'

'No problem there. We'll bring her out to live with us. I can tack on another room at the back of the house, and she'll be snug as a bug in a rug. She'll be company for you in the long winter nights, too. What do you think?'

Paula had a wild vision of Lydia living in a lean-to on the prairie, far away from civilisation and everything that she knew and loved. She almost laughed at the thought, but it was not her mother's company that she was hoping for in those winter evenings.

She took a deep breath.

'I'm sorry, Jake, but the answer still has to be no. I feel greatly honoured by your proposal, but I know it wouldn't work out. We're two very different people. No, let me finish,' she said, holding up a hand to stop him as he began to interrupt. 'I've seen what is required of these prairie women, and I know I could never measure up to them. I'd try, but I don't know how to do most things that Annie and the rest do on a daily basis. I'd fail you, Jake, and that wouldn't be right.'

'You could learn, couldn't you, same as you did with them cakes?'

She shook her head.

'I'm afraid the little English rose is just too soft for this way of life. I'm sorry, Jake, and I do hope you don't feel that I've led you on. For a while I did wonder if I could manage to stay, but I see now that I was expecting too much of myself.'

Jake stood up, scratching his head.

'Well, it was worth a try. No harm in asking, I thought.'

'No harm at all. Will you be all right?'

'Me? Oh, yes. As it happens I've a distant cousin back East. She has a girl about your age, and she's willing to take me on, sight-unseen. Molly, I mean, not the mother. I believe I'll tell her to come ahead. We can get wed before spring planting time comes.'

* * *

'I've never heard anything like it in all my life!' Paula spluttered when her beau had departed. 'To think that I'm only one of the women on his list! It was all I could do not to tell him what I really thought of him, and it was only for Peter's sake that I kept quiet. He was sitting in the corner all that time, quiet as a mouse, and looking anxious.'

'At least you have the satisfaction of knowing you were top of his list,' Annie pointed out.

'And now some poor girl he's never even met is willing to come out here to fill his first wife's shoes? I just can't take it in.'

'As for that, it wouldn't be the first time that a mail-order bride has come to these parts.'

'A mail-order bride! What on earth is that?'

'Oh, the newspapers back East are full of advertisements for wives, Paula. I remember seeing them before we moved out here. Unattached women are a rarity here, and it's a lonely existence for a bachelor trying to clear the land and make a living for himself without a wife to look after him. Then there are widowers, such as Jake Marriott. What are they supposed to do if a wife ups and dies on them, leaving them with little ones to raise? Better a marriage of convenience than the alternative.'

'But it's all so grim, Annie. Where's the romance?'

'Romance is for them that can afford it, my girl. Real life isn't all moonlight and roses, you know.'

'I think I'm just beginning to find that out.'

Still, she stubbornly clung to her old ideals. There was plenty of room in the world for love and laughter. Her romantic soul yearned for her share of those. Relieved of the necessity to consider a possible future as Mrs Jake Marriott she suddenly felt more light-hearted than she had done since leaving Wimbledon. Better things were just around the corner. Maybe!

Meeting Lola

'That man is here again,' Anna Mae lisped. 'He's in the barn, talking to Dad.'

Paula's heart gave an uncomfortable lurch. What now? Had Jake decided to try again? Had Molly decided not to come after all?

She looked to Annie for help.

'Don't leave me alone with him! I don't want to be fast-talked into anything. I've made up my mind, and that's the end of it.'

'It's not him, Paula,' Annie hissed, trying to see past the fern-like frost on the kitchen window. 'It's the other one!'

'What other one?'

'You know, that cousin of yours.'

'It can't be!' Paula ran to the window, so full of joy she thought her heart might burst from her chest.

Charles was muffled to the chin in an

enormous beaver coat, which he must have purchased in Calgary, for she had never seen it before.

'I'll make you some tea and then I'm going out to the barn,' Annie said firmly. 'If another proposal is coming, I don't wish to hear it!'

But she was smiling as she spoke.

'Charles! What a surprise!'

'A nice one, I hope.'

'Of course it's lovely to see you. Let me take your coat. Then you can tell me all your news.'

'The main news is that Lola and I have broken off our engagement.'

'Charles! What happened? I thought you were happily planning the wedding.'

'Lola's mother was. The bride-to-be and her father have other ideas.'

'I don't understand.'

'You know that Mr King is a businessman, with a number of irons in the fire. His original idea was to visit Canada for a few months to see to business interests here, before returning to England. Now he intends to remain in Canada for an indefinite period, because he feels that Calgary is the city of the future. It has grown so rapidly these last few years that he can see endless possibilities for him to add to his wealth.'

'But how does that affect you?'

'Lola has persuaded her father to offer me a job here as chief solicitor to his firm.'

'Gosh!'

'The only problem is that it's not for me. Canada is a wonderful country but I'm an Englishman through and through. I want to continue my life in Gloucester, Paula. Besides, I'm trained in English law, and things are different here.'

'So you turned him down, and then what happened?'

'Lola threw the biggest tantrum of all time, throwing herself about hysterically and shouting that I don't care about her, for if I did I would do what she wants. She wouldn't have it when I tried to explain. Then she started to complain about you, Paula. According to her, I've been neglecting her shamefully by running out here to make sure you're all right. 'A simple little music teacher', she called you, Paula. Well I wasn't having that! A wife can't criticise a chap's relatives. It's just not on!'

'It's a good thing she doesn't know that we're not blood relatives at all. Don't worry, Charles. I'm sure you'll be able to patch things up when you go back.'

'I have no wish to patch things up, as you put it. The scales have fallen from my eyes, Paula. Lola and I were never right for each other. I fell for a pretty face and a charming manner, but that is no basis for marriage. I can't be doing with someone who sulks and pouts whenever she can't get her own way.'

'How did she react when you ended the engagement?'

'Oh, that was her doing. She flung the ring at me and said she didn't want to marry a man who trampled all over her feelings like a mad bull at the Calgary Stampede. Her mother was in the background bleating about the wedding plans and how the dress was already made, but I took no notice. I put the ring into my wallet and went upstairs to pack. And here I am.'

'I'm sorry.' It was a lie, but one had to observe the conventions, after all.

'I'm not. I'm thankful the wretched girl saved me the embarrassment of having to break it off myself. But that's enough about me, Paula. Is there a wedding in your future?'

'I'm afraid not.'

'Your chap didn't come up to scratch, then?'

'He did propose, but I've turned him down.'

'That must have been awkward for you.'

'Not really. He's already found somebody else, as it happens.'

Charles lifted an eyebrow.

'Quick work, wouldn't you say?'

'Things are different out here on the prairie,' Paula sighed.

'So where does this leave you? Have you signed on to continue teaching here?'

'Again, the answer is no. I've been replaced by somebody's niece.'

Charles steepled his fingers together, looking very much the lawyer advising a difficult client.

'Then you don't seem to have any other options, do you, old girl?'

'Well, I've decided that I'd better do as Mother wants, and return to England. I'll have no regrets. This has been a wonderful experience, the holiday of a lifetime. I'm ready to settle down now and become a maiden aunt to Bertie's children, if he ever has any. Of course, I can't sail for England just now, so I'm considering two options. I can either go to Calgary and try to find a job there, and a place to live, or I can stay on in this house as a paying guest. Annie has already offered me that, bless her kind heart.'

'There is a third option, you know.'

'What's that?'

'You can come with me to Ottawa.'

'Ottawa?' Paula was intrigued by the thought.

'Like you, I have to wait until the first ship leaves in the spring. I'd like to see a bit more of the country while I'm here, and Ottawa should be interesting, being the capital. I'll travel by train, as before, only in reverse. I'd love you to travel with me. We'll be company for each other, and when we get to the other end I can help you find a respectable place to stay and make sure you don't get rooked by an unscrupulous landlady.'

'All right, I'll do it! What do we do next?'

Smiling, Charles leaned forward and took her hands in his.

'You'll come back to Calgary with me tonight, and we'll look up the train times first thing in the morning. How does that sound?'

'It's getting dark, Charles. It really

isn't safe to go tramping across the prairie on a winter's night. We could die before we ever reach the city. They'll find us in the morning, frozen stiff like a pair of icicles.'

'I'm sure that's an exaggeration.'

'Then what about my trunk? Are we going to drag that behind us through the snow?'

Fortunately Annie was able to resolve the situation.

'Of course you can't go wandering off at this time of night!' she insisted. 'Can they, Brian? We'll put you up for the night, Mr Ingram — you can have Anna Mae's bed and she'll come in with us.'

'And in the morning I'll harness up the sleigh and take you to the station,' Brian added.

After a happy evening playing croki-nole and checkers with the Maxwells, Paula retired for the night, feeling happier than she had done for many a long day. She was about to journey far away with the man of her dreams, leaving the unpleasant Lola behind them. Could life get any better?

Once back in Calgary Paula and Charles spent a quiet Christmas at the Balmoral Hotel. At first the manager seemed disinclined to accommodate them, saying they were fully booked, which Paula interpreted as a ploy to discourage them from staying. She suspected that the staff were hoping to have time off over the holidays, or at least to have time to themselves for their own jollifications.

Charles was equal to the occasion.

'I don't know how you dared to threaten him with legal action as you did,' Paula said admiringly when they were sitting in the room she was allocated, Charles's quarters being further down the hall. 'He must know that you don't have any jurisdiction in this country.'

'It wasn't that,' Charles said. 'It was when he suggested that he might be able to find us something if we greased his palm. I wasn't having that! I mentioned Mr King's name — everyone here has heard of him by now — and suggested that he would be happy to contact the owner of the hotel, who in turn would be interested to know what is going on here.'

'And so he suddenly remembered that they had a cancellation,' Paula agreed, bouncing on the side of the bed, which seemed comfortable enough. 'Thank goodness you were with me, Charles. I don't know how I'd have managed if you hadn't been here to speak up. What should we have done if they really hadn't had a vacancy?'

'I suppose we could have gone back to the Kings',' Charles said, with a shrug.

Paula shuddered to think of the reception they would have received from Lola and her mother. Even the hospitable Samuel King would probably have shown them the door in a hurry.

'I'll book us on the first transcontinental train that's scheduled to leave after Christmas,' he went on. 'We'll be in Ottawa by this time next week. We'll find conditions there more to our liking, I expect. Most of Ontario was settled something like a century ago, so it's comparatively civilised.'

'Mother will be glad to know we're on our way home,' Paula said. 'Even though we'll be in Ottawa until the spring, we'll be a couple of thousand miles closer to England. I'll write to her this evening and let her know what's happening.'

'She'll be happy to hear that you've turned down Marriott's proposal to turn you into a prairie wife.'

'Mother doesn't know about that, and if you happen to write to her, please don't say a word about it. If I'd accepted Jake's proposal I'd have had to break the news sooner or later, but as things stand there's no need to mention it now. I suppose I'll tell her some day, but there's no point in upsetting her unnecessarily now.'

On Christmas Eve they attended the

midnight service at a fashionable little church in the city, arriving early so as to be sure of a seat. Paula enjoyed watching the fashionably dressed women who probably represented Calgary's elite.

She stiffened suddenly.

'Don't look now, Charles! There are the Kings!'

Charles, of course, looked up at once. Fortunately the Kings didn't notice him. They swept past on their way to a front row pew, escorted by a sidesman.

Samuel King carried his top hat in one hand; his other hand was under his wife's elbow as he steered her carefully down the aisle. Mrs King's dress, or what Paula could see of it, was of heavily ribbed dark-blue silk. Over this she wore an expensive-looking seal coat with a silk scarf protruding from the pocket.

Lola had evidently dressed to be seen, for she carried her coat over her arm. An elegant dress of burgundy wool was on display to anyone who cared to look and it had been made in the new shorter style so that the girl's smart black boots were clearly visible.

Charles's expression was impossible to read. Was he regretting his broken engagement? He had loved Lola for a long time. Paula was thankful when the procession started down the aisle and the congregation rose to sing the opening hymn.

When the service was over, Charles made no move to leave the church, obviously waiting until the Kings had left the building. Lola appeared not to notice them as she swept past, but then she would not have expected to see them here. Paula held her breath until the girl was out of sight.

She did not feel completely safe until, two days after Christmas, they were seated on the train. Even then, she anxiously regarded all the other passengers as they made their way up the aisle. It would be just her luck if the Kings had also decided to travel east and she was forced to encounter them on board. Thankfully they did not appear, and she sat back, prepared to enjoy herself.

She made friends with a young woman of about her own age, Mavis Lyons, who was returning to Ottawa with her husband.

'This beats the train we came out on,' she said, looking about her with appreciation as they sipped strong tea in the dining car.

'Why, did you come on a goods train?' Paula asked, by way of a joke.

'A what?'

'You know, a train that carries goods to market or something.'

'Oh, you mean a freight train. No, we didn't, but we came on a harvest excursion, and that's almost as bad!'

'How is that different?'

'Well, those are special trains that bring workers out West to help with the harvest. There's good money to be made there, if you can stand the pace. The thing is, the harvest trains are pretty basic. They have a stove in each carriage and you have to cook your own food on them in sweltering heat. Never again, I can tell you! We stayed on because my Jack thought he could get labouring work out here, but it didn't work out. No connections, you see. If you didn't have some 'in' with the bosses you were out of luck. What were you doing out here?'

'I've been teaching school on the prairie. Near a place called Lyman's Creek.'

'Never heard of it.'

'I don't suppose many people have.'

'Why give it up, a nice clean occupation like that?'

'The chairman of the school trustees wanted the job for his niece.'

It was as convenient a reason as any; she really didn't wish to discuss her love life with a stranger, nor to share Bertie's story.

'It's the same thing all over the world.' Her new friend sighed. 'It's who you know, isn't it? It doesn't matter how good you are at your job, there's always someone waiting to pull you down.'

Paula could hardly agree with this gloomy view of life, but then she realised how sheltered she had been in Wimbledon, with money and family behind her.

'I say,' Mavis said suddenly: 'who's that gorgeous fellow that just came in?'

Paula craned her neck and saw that Charles had just arrived.

'That's my cousin, Charles,' she explained.

'Your cousin! You didn't say you have a cousin. I thought you were travelling alone.'

'He's been staying in Calgary, but he's heading back to England now, so it suits us both to travel together.'

'Aren't you going to introduce me?'

Paula was proud of the way that Charles swung into polite conversation with Mavis, treating the girl in the manner with which he might engage ladies in a polite exchange in Lydia's drawing-room, rather than a stranger on a train. That must come from dealing with clients in his law office, of course. He had acquired a professional air of quiet competence that must serve him well back in Gloucester.

'I must find my husband,' Mavis said at last, getting to her feet. 'I don't suppose you've seen a tall, red-headed man anywhere? Sun-tanned, with a scar on his face?'

'Actually, yes, I did see such a man, back in the last carriage before the caboose. There seemed to be a poker game going on.'

Mavis gasped.

'If he's lost all our savings I'll never speak to him again!' She rushed off, colliding with a passing waiter in the process.

'Poor woman,' Paula said. 'She's had a hard life, and if her husband is a gambler into the bargain I can see the reason why. Just what is a caboose?'

'The guard's van, to you. And I suspect that your Mr Marriott is something of a gambler, too.'

'He is not!' Paula leaped to Jake's defence. She may not have wanted to marry the man, but he was a decent good-living individual, and for Charles to think badly of him would have reflected on her own judgment.

Charles grinned.

'Simmer down, old girl! All I meant was, he must be a bit of a betting man to take a chance on this unknown girl he means to marry. The same goes for all the other chaps who send for mail-order brides. What happens if one of them finds out he's made a mistake? Marriage is for life. Once a man has made that commitment there's nothing he can do about it but soldier on. He can't return a wife to her parents like an unwanted package delivered by mistake!'

'You could have ended up in just that situation if you hadn't seen the light in time,' Paula wanted to say. But she managed to bite her tongue.

As they sped through the night, Paula sat beside Charles in the darkened carriage, quietly rocking to the motion of the train. Charles had hired a heavy plaid wool travelling-rug which he had spread over their knees, and she revelled in his nearness. He fell asleep before she did, and she wished this moment could last for ever. All around them other people were settling down for the night, pummelling pillows into shape or making last-minute trips to the water closet.

Paula wondered what Mother was doing now. If her calculations were correct it must be mid-morning in Wimbledon. Lydia might be entertaining guests to tea, or out paying calls if the weather was suitable. As for Bertie, what was he up to? Was he still playing Sherlock Holmes, or had he already tired of that and moved on to something more congenial?

She resolved to write to him the next day. She might or might not receive an answer, of course; you could never rely on Bertie to do the right thing. On the other hand, he owed her a very large favour, so he might feel compelled to respond.

She would also write to Elsie, who was carrying a very large burden at the moment, taking on Paula's responsibilities at the house as well as her own. A letter of appreciation could make all the difference between Elsie keeping up the good work or handing in her notice, if driven too far!

Paula awoke with a jerk as the train came to a shuddering halt. She realised that without meaning to she had been asleep in Charles's arms. His right arm was around her and her head was resting on his shoulder. For a moment she remained where she was, half dazed. This felt so right, so very much as things were meant to be. She knew without a fraction of a doubt that they were meant to be together for the rest of their lives.

Then reality set in and she moved away from his unwitting embrace, blinking back tears.

Charles yawned and stretched.

'What's going on? Why have we stopped? Is this a station?' Other people were asking the same question.

'No problem,' the conductor assured them. 'We're snowed in, that's all. It's been coming down all night. I reckon we've seen at least two feet of the white stuff. There's nothing to worry about, ladies and gentlemen. We'll soon have it cleared and then we'll be on our way.'

'How on earth are they going to do that?' Paula wondered. 'Do they have some sort of machine for clearing snow?'

She was soon to find out. A group of men dressed in heavy overalls and flat caps got busy with shovels, tossing the heavy snow aside as if it was feather-light.

'That's the section gang,' the conductor explained. 'The railroad is divided into sections, each with a foreman and groups of men whose job it is to look after their few miles of track, summer and winter.'

'It seems a hard way to make a

living,' Charles murmured sympathetically.

'It's tradition in many families along the line,' the conductor rejoined. 'Fathers and sons and cousins, all doing the same job, and glad to get it. That's how I started out, sir, before I got the chance to come on board as a brakeman. Now, as you see, I've come up in the world!'

'They must have similar employees on British railways,' Paula decided, 'but I've never seen them.'

'You've never seen snow like this, either,' Charles said.

'This is eerie,' Paula said, peering out of the window at the grey dawn sky. I hope we're not stuck here for long.'

'What does it matter? We're not going anywhere in particular.'

'What about our reservations at the hotel? They might not hold them if we don't show up.'

'We're booked in at the Château Laurier in Ottawa. You're forgetting that it's run by the railroad. They must be used to delays.' He put his arm around her again. 'Now, then, snuggle down and go back to sleep. When you wake up it will be breakfast time and you can get a nice cup of tea.'

So, he was aware that she had slept in his arms! Paula leaned back in her seat. Was he beginning to see her as something more than just a cousin? If only that were true! What would happen if she were to make her feelings plain to Charles? She wasn't like Lola, who simpered and flounced and made men sit up and take notice. Paula had never been any good at flirting.

If she tried fluttering her eyelashes at Charles he'd probably ask her if she had something in her eye. Apart from the fathers and husbands of her music pupils she had never had anything to do with men. Her only experience of interacting with the opposite sex had been Bertie. With him she had spoken out naturally, always saying what was on her mind.

Could she do the same with Charles?

She knew that was impossible.

A proper English miss in this year of 1912 was expected to be prim and proper, letting the man make the first move. Charles would be alarmed and disgusted if she told him what was in her heart and mind.

'I love you, Charles, I've loved you since I was a little girl and you brought me pails of water to make a moat around my sandcastle. I loved you when you used to come down from Oxford in the long vac, telling us all about your adventures during the term. Most of all I realised it when I saw how patient and kind you were with that awful Lola.'

She could go on and say how she knew they were right for each other. How she hoped they could make a life together, bringing up children, enjoying grandchildren, growing old together. But she shied away from the thought. What was the point in torturing herself?

'What's the matter with you?'

'Me? Nothing. Why do you ask?'

'You seemed a bit doleful there.

You're not worried about Aunt Lydia, are you? I'm sure she'll be all right now that Cousin Bertie is back with her.'

'Mother? I expect I'll hear from her soon. In fact, I hope there will be a letter waiting when we reach the hotel. I posted one off to her before we left Calgary, giving her my address in Ottawa. Now, if you'll excuse me, I want to go along to the ladies' room and tidy myself up. I can't think what I look like.'

'Beautiful as ever,' Charles said gallantly.

Engaged!

The Château Laurier was another of the CPR hotels, although not as fairylike as its counterpart in Quebec City, Paula decided. She stood in the foyer, waiting while Charles dealt with the business of checking into the hotel. She was looking about her at the opulence of the place and wondering how long they could afford to stay here, when she heard a familiar voice.

'Well, hello! We met in Quebec, didn't we?'

'Er, yes, I believe we did,' Paula said, struggling to recall if she knew the woman's name. Amelia somebody, wasn't it? A first-class bore, and nosey with it.

'Is that your brother over there at the reception desk? Such a handsome man! I thought you said you were going to Calgary to meet him, but I could have sworn he was with you at Quebec!'

'Actually, that is my cousin. We're travelling together.'

'Yes? So where is this brother of yours, then?'

Paula longed to tell the woman to mind her own business, but she had been brought up to be polite, and old habits died hard.

'Bertie has already returned to England. Our mother isn't very well and we felt that one of us should be with her.'

'Very right and proper, but surely it's a daughter's place to do that! How must the poor woman feel, thinking of her daughter gadding all over a foreign country, enjoying herself?'

Now this beastly woman had gone too far!

'Actually I've been teaching at a school in the west. I would have gone home sooner but the ships don't sail at this time of year, as you're no doubt aware.'

Amelia's beady eyes swivelled to the

desk, where Charles was pointing out his luggage to a young man in pageboy costume.

'I wonder how your poor mother feels about your travelling with a man?'

'Charles is my cousin!' Paula snapped. 'Not that this is any of your concern, thank you very much!'

'Cousins have been known to marry,' the awful woman went on, not deterred in the slightest by Paula's icy glare.

'Exactly, and that is what we plan to do. I am engaged to Charles, and I might point out that he is a solicitor and will take legal action if you attempt to spread unpleasant rumours about us.'

'There's no need to get up on your high horse, missy! I'm only thinking of your reputation, you know. Any breath of scandal could taint your cousin's career, and you should be aware of that. I'm sure your dear mother would tell you the same, if she were here.'

'Come along, Paula. The boy is waiting to show us to our rooms.'

Charles! How long had he been standing there? What had he heard? By the way he emphasised that last word she knew that he had heard at least part of her conversation with Amelia.

She made no attempt to introduce the pair. Let the wretched woman think what she liked! Paula's reputation was already in tatters as far as she was concerned. Fortunately there was no way that her sly innuendos and nasty gibes could reach the ears of anyone in the Scotts' social circle.

'We'll meet in the dining-room for lunch, shall we?' Charles suggested when he left her at the door of her room. 'Or are you too tired? You can order up room service instead if you prefer. I shan't mind.'

'Is that what you mean to do?'

'Room service? No, I think I'd rather sit at a proper table in the dining-room. With my fiancée,' he said, not meeting her eye.

Paula's face turned the colour of ripe strawberries.

'That awful woman!' she blurted out. 'I had to say something to shut her up!'

'We'll discuss this later,' he said, turning to leave.

Mortified, she opened the door and went into her room.

Having exchanged her crumpled blouse for a clean one and attended to her face and hair, Paula felt ready to face the music. She marched into the dining-room, head held high, pleased to see that Charles was already at their table. He stood up at her approach and carefully helped her to take her place. A hovering waiter joined them at once.

'Would you care to see the wine list, sir?'

'No, thank you. I think we're ready to look at the menu, please.'

'Very good, sir.' The sommelier beckoned to another waiter, who approached, carrying two leather-covered bills of fare.

Paula would have liked a glass of wine, to fortify herself for what was ahead, but she could hardly say so.

Shaking inwardly she agreed to Charles's suggestion that they start with mock turtle soup, followed by lamb chops with mint and duchesse potatoes.

'About what I said before,' she began, when the waiter had departed.

'Not while we're eating, Paula. Wait until we're relaxing in the lounge after luncheon. I've taken a look around and there's an enormous fire burning in the fireplace there. We can sit there and chat in comfort.'

Paula scarcely tasted any of the delicious food that was placed in front of her by the attentive waiter. When the dessert trolley appeared at her side she shook her head despite the enticing array of sweet goods which were presented for her inspection.

As Charles had said, a wonderful log fire was burning in the lounge grate, occasionally sending out a shower of blue sparks. Paula sank down in a chintz-covered armchair, stretching out her hands towards the warmth.

'Charles,' she began. 'What you heard . . . '

'We meet again!' The awful Amelia appeared at her side. 'I'm afraid we haven't been introduced, but I want you to meet my husband.'

The large, red-faced man stuck out his hand in Charles's direction.

'Joseph Dinwiddie, at your service. I believe you're already acquainted with my wife, Amelia.'

Charles stood up and bowed to Mrs Dinwiddie.

'Won't you sit down, Mrs Dinwiddie.'

'I believe I will,' she said, sliding into the chair next to him. 'I wanted to congratulate you on your engagement to your lovely cousin here.'

'Thank you, madam.'

'It's funny, but when we met back in Quebec City I somehow thought you were engaged to another young lady!'

'Did you?' Charles countered. 'How odd.'

Mrs Dinwiddie was only briefly disconcerted.

'You must tell me all about your wedding plans, Miss Scott. And do let me see your ring!' She reached over and took hold of Paula's ringless left hand.

'Oh, dear, I see you're not wearing it. I hope you haven't lost it! Train travel is so difficult, isn't it? Nowhere to put anything for safety, not like on board ship where you can leave your valuables with the purser.'

'We haven't purchased the ring yet,' Charles told her. 'We couldn't find anything suitable in Calgary, but I understand that Ottawa has some very fine shops. You'll find that Paula is wearing a sign of her attachment to me in a very short time.'

Watching the Dinwiddies as they walked towards the door, Paula could hardly believe the charade that had just played out. What on earth had Charles been up to? Obviously he had wanted to protect her from the vicious tongue of the scandalmongering woman, but now Amelia Dinwiddie wouldn't give up until she'd seen a ring on Paula's finger!

Paula remembered the impressive diamond solitaire that had adorned Lola's finger. What had become of that? She had a vague idea that when an engagement was broken off, the ring had to be returned to the gentleman who had purchased it.

So was that ring now reposing in Charles's pocket? Did he intend to let Paula wear it, in order to put Amelia off the scent?

'I won't do it!' she told herself fiercely.

* * *

The following day was fine, if bitterly cold, and Charles and Paula set out on foot, determined to see something of Ottawa. It was not as old as Quebec City and historic old stone buildings were few and far between, but the view from Parliament Hill made up for that. The parliament buildings were indeed made of stone, with copper roofs that showed green in the sun. Far below them, the icebound Ottawa River stretched into the distance, much wider than the Thames at home.

'I wish we were going to be here in late spring,' Charles said. 'I've been reading up about this river and it seems that the lumbermen float logs down it as far as Montreal and Quebec City. There's a picture in my guidebook of a big raft passing by, complete with cookhouse on board. That raft is made up of square timbers being sent to Europe. They dismantle the rafts when they reach the ports.'

'Fancy!'

'Of course they can't do that in winter because the river freezes over. Look over there, Paula. There's something you won't see in England!'

Paula looked past his outstretched and saw two horse-drawn sleighs venturing down the bank, filled with laughing people.

'We've got to stop them!' she gasped. 'Do something, Charles! Whatever can they be thinking off? They'll all be drowned, and I can't bear to watch them!'

He laughed.

'Apparently there's nothing to worry about at this time of year. They told me at the hotel that the ice is at least three-feet thick, quite strong enough to hold up an army! Why don't we go for a walk over the ice? It would be something to talk about when we get back to England.'

Paula shuddered.

'Count me out! In any case I'm getting cold. I'd love to get out of this wind.'

'Right, then! We'll go back down to Sparks Street and find a jeweller's shop. Its time we had a look for that ring!'

'No, Charles! We don't have to do that.'

'We most certainly do.'

'But I can't see why we should play up to that woman! What does she matter to us?'

'I spoke to her husband in the billiard

room. It seems the Dinwiddies have numerous friends and relations in England, including London. You see how Amelia loves to gossip, and I'm sure she'd like to drop in some salacious details when she next writes home. Can't you imagine it? 'We have a young couple staying here who like to pretend they are cousins, but I don't believe a word of it! Such a scandal, my dear, and him a solicitor, too. Definitely not the sort of person I'd trust with my private business, I can tell you! Chap named Ingram. He comes from Gloucester. Have you heard of him?' '

'I thought it was my reputation you were trying to protect!'

'Certainly it is, but I have to think of my own good name as well. If spiteful rumours get back to my partners in Gloucester it won't do my career much good.'

As if in a dream Paula followed Charles down the street until they came to a shop that displayed a number of expensive-looking items of jewellery in the window. When he opened the door, to the accompaniment of a melodious chime, she stepped inside obediently.

'I wish to purchase an engagement ring,' Charles told the elderly man who came forward to greet them. 'May we see a selection?'

'Certainly, sir. We have some very fine stones in stock, or we can always have a ring made up for you, if you prefer.'

Paula wondered what their policy was on taking back unwanted rings, for surely Charles didn't mean to waste good money on a ring that was only for show?

'I'd prefer not to have a diamond,' she murmured, thinking of the ostentatious stone that Lola had displayed. 'Do you have something more colourful? A garnet, perhaps?'

Charles frowned, but he nodded to the man who replaced the tray of diamond solitaires and brought out a different selection.

Paula left the shop wearing a very fine ring featuring a row of three rubies in a crown setting.

Sailing Home

'How long shall we stay at the Château Laurier?' she asked, when they were walking back to the hotel, huddled inside their coats against the biting wind.

'Why? Don't you like it there?'

'Of course I do, but it must be so expensive. It's not a bit like a railway hotel in Britain, is it? At this rate I'll have spent everything I earned teaching school long before it's time to sail back to England. And, please,' she went on, lifting a hand to prevent an interruption, 'don't say that you will pay for me. I can't allow that. We must find somewhere less expensive to stay.'

'I am not prepared to stay in some cheap boarding-house, Paula. I'm not penniless and I came to Canada prepared to stay for some weeks.'

'Staying with the Kings,' she couldn't

resist pointing out.

'That's true, but I was expecting to pay my way when it came to other things, such as escorting Lola to social events, and then coming East before we sailed for England as I fully expected to do. That much has not changed. I have cabled my bank for more funds. No doubt I shall have to begin again to replenish my savings but in the meantime I can live quite comfortably here.'

'I don't have savings,' Paula muttered, regretting now that she had spent the money received from her piano pupils on frivolities such as silk stockings and scented soap. 'If I borrow from you I'll never be able to pay it back.'

Charles smiled.

'I have written to your family solicitor, Paula, asking that a sum of money be released from the family trusts, enough to cover your expenses here. He will arrange a letter of credit for you.'

'Bertie won't like that!'

'Bertie will have to put up with it. If it were not for his irresponsible behaviour you would not be stranded here now. And, while we're on the subject, I have a word or two to say about Aunt Lydia. I know that she is your mother, Paula, but it was very foolish of her to send you out here on a wild goose chase! It would have been far better to leave Bertie to find his own way out of his muddle. He has to grow up some time. Naturally she was concerned about the boy, but what about your wellbeing? Is that to be sacrificed for your brother's sake?'

Paula stared at Charles in surprise. She had never known him to be so vehement.

'I'm glad she did send me out here. In fact, I jumped at the chance! You can have no idea of the dull lives we daughters lead at home while you men can go and conquer the world. I don't suppose I'll ever have a holiday like this again. Brighton or Bognor Regis will be the limit of my experience.'

Charles smiled at this, taking her remark as the joke she had intended it to be, but all the same there was an element of truth in it. Spending time in the world's most romantic city with Charles — or with any man, come to that — was as unlikely to happen as seeing polar bears in Wimbledon. And that, as any fool would know, was nothing but a fantasy.

Letters awaited them when they returned to the hotel. Paula was pleased to find one from Annie, who had penned several pages of local gossip.

We've got that new school teacher, and what a pain she's turning out to be! It's our turn to board her and she complains about every little thing — her bedroom is too draughty; she can't eat cabbage; isn't there something more interesting to do in the evenings; playing board games is for children. Truly, Paula, I think I shall go mad before the month is over. Do write back at once and tell me all your doings.

Paula turned the page over.

I hope this won't upset you, but Jake Marriott is married. The bride seems a nice enough girl, although too young to be much of a friend for most of the women here. They tied the knot in our church and we all took food for the reception afterwards. Young Peter doesn't seem too pleased with his new mama but I suppose he'll get used to her in time.

Jake was married! Paula was pleased to realise that the news did not upset her at all.

'I've had a nice letter from my friend, Annie,' she told Charles, who looked up from his own letter with a frown on his face. 'What's the matter, Charles? Not bad news, I hope?'

'It's from Lola.'

Paula experienced an uncomfortable feeling in the pit of her stomach.

'What does she have to say?'

'Basically, come back, all is forgiven.'

'Oh.'

'Her father has repeated his offer of a

job, at a salary far beyond my original expectations. Lola says that she is prepared to forgive me for my horrid behaviour, as she puts it, and if I will return at once we can take up where we left off. Apparently nobody has been told about our broken engagement and people are starting to ask about wedding arrangements.'

'What are you going to do?'

'I don't know. I shall have to think.' He jumped to his feet and dashed out of the room.

Paula was left alone by the fire. Twisting the ruby ring on her third finger she tried to assess the situation. Would he go back to Lola? He had loved her once. Could the embers of that love be fanned into flames once more?

As a not-totally-disinterested observer, she could see what was happening here. Lola had broken off the engagement in a fit of pique, probably intending to bend Charles to her will by doing so. When that didn't happen she hadn't had the grace to apologise and he had left. Now she wanted him back, if only because people were asking when the wedding was to take place and she didn't want to lose face. She had appealed to Papa, whose money might be able to buy back her fiancé for her.

Paula curled her lip in disgust. Samuel King might be an astute businessman, but he had no wisdom where his spoiled young daughter was concerned. She glanced down at her ruby ring again. With the arrival of that letter her own dream had turned into nightmare. What would Charles decide to do?

'Is that the ring? Do let me see!' Paula started at the sound of the piercing voice that came from somewhere behind her. Amelia Dinwiddie, of course.

Suppressing a sigh she held out her left hand for the annoying woman's inspection.

'He didn't buy you a diamond, then!'

'I don't care for diamonds, Mrs

Dinwiddie. Rubies are more colourful, don't you think?'

'I suppose so, but for an engagement? Well, you know best, I suppose. Now, then, tell me all about it. Do you mean to be married here in Ottawa? A winter wedding will be lovely. You must make your husband buy you a white fur coat, my dear. So bride-like!'

'We couldn't have the wedding here, Mrs Dinwiddie. My mother would never forgive me if she couldn't be present to see me married. And then there's my brother. He'll expect to give me away, because our father is dead.'

'So the wedding will have to wait until you return to England. Where will it take place? I believe that your fiancé is from Gloucester? Such a lovely old town. I have a distant cousin there — Emily Sutton. Have you heard of her? I must write to tell her all about you, so she can make your acquaintance after you settle in. If she ever needs a solicitor she will know whom to approach.'

Paula longed to get rid of the wretched woman. If Mrs Dinwiddie ever found out that Charles had been engaged to the lovely Lola King prior to entering into a completely make-believe engagement to Paula the fat would really be in the fire. The gong sounded for luncheon, and Charles did not appear. Paula went to the dining-room, choosing a table that gave her a view of the reception desk. She wondered if Charles was even now booking a place on the next train to Calgary. She ordered a Waldorf salad but she only toyed with it when it came.

Later, after peering into each of the public rooms on the ground floor of the hotel, she discovered Charles in the writing-room. He was hunched over a leather-tooled desk and, to judge by the number of crumpled sheets that filled the waste-paper basket, he had met with little success in his task.

'Hello, Charles. Are you writing to Lola?'

He jerked into an upright position.

'Paula? Sorry, I must have nodded off.'

'It is warm in here. Did you know you missed luncheon?'

'I wasn't hungry.'

'Neither was I. What have you been doing?'

'Isn't it obvious? I'm attempting to reply to Lola's letter, of course, and not getting very far.'

'As I see it, you have two choices. Either you point out that your engagement is over and you've moved on with your life, or you let her know that you'll be back at her side as soon as possible.'

'It's not as easy as that.'

'I don't see why not. Do you want her back?'

'I do not. I must have been an absolute fool to be taken in by her. And what sort of marriage would it be if I could be bribed into going through with it against my better judgment?'

'Exactly.'

'But, Paula, you must see that I can't tell her that, or at least, not in so many words. I have no wish to hurt her feelings. Perhaps it will be best if I go out to Calgary and tell her face to face.'

'Where she will try to wheedle you into doing what she wants. Can't you see that this is just what she's hoping for?'

'You're very harsh, Paula.'

'You're probably right. Never mind me. This is none of my business. You must do as you think best.' Blinking back hot tears she fled from the room, hardly knowing where she was going, or even caring.

Charles wasn't the only fool here. Why couldn't she just tell him how she felt about him? Why wasn't she prepared to fight for him, instead of letting him play into Lola's greedy hands?

One problem, at least, was resolved that evening, when Charles was called to the telephone. Paula watched anxiously as he stood in the kiosk in the entrance hall, gesticulating now and then. When at last he emerged she ran to his side, desperate to know what was happening.

'I hope it's not bad news, is it? It's not Mother, or Bertie?'

For a moment he didn't reply and she tugged at his sleeve.

'I hope there's nothing wrong in Gloucester, is there? Something to do with the practice?'

'No, no,' he said, looking at her in a dazed sort of way. 'Nothing like that. If you must know, it was Samuel King.'

'Lola's father!'

'Apparently Lola has worked herself up into a fine state. She's shut herself in her room and refuses to eat. They've had to get the doctor in, and he's diagnosed female hysteria, whatever that is.'

'Just another word for a tantrum,' Paula replied before she could stop herself.

'Mama is frantic, of course, and the pair of them have prevailed upon Mr King to speak to me. He's offered me an even greater financial inducement if

I'll make it up with Lola.'

'And shall you?'

'Certainly not! What basis for marriage would there be if Lola knew she could always get her own way by throwing a fit, or running to Papa? I mistook her manipulative ways for a playful nature. Now I see that marriage to Lola King would have been a nightmare and I've had a lucky escape.'

'I hope you didn't tell her father that!'

'No. I was as tactful as possible. I laid all the blame on myself. Too devoted to my work, too set in my ways, so on and so forth. Poor little Lola would find herself neglected while I forced my way up the ladder of success.'

'Did he believe you?'

'Who knows? He accepted it in the end, though he must know in his heart that his daughter is a spoiled little girl who would never succeed as the wife of a Gloucester solicitor. Why, the local matrons would snub her if she tried to rule the roost, and Papa's money would not buy her entry into society there.'

'Poor Lola,' Paula said, meaning it for once. 'Still, with her looks and Daddy's money she'll soon find someone else.'

The remaining weeks of winter passed quickly. The banks of snow on the streets began to collapse into dirty puddles, and the people gradually left off their gloves and fur hats. Charles confirmed their passage on the Cunard ship that would make the first Atlantic crossing of 1913, and Paula contacted her mother to let her know the arrangements.

I should like Bertie to meet me at Southampton, to help me make my way back to Wimbledon with my baggage. Charles will be going directly to Gloucester, and I can't expect him to do more for me than he has already. There are porters, of course, but women always seem to be invisible where such men are concerned, and I cannot handle my trunk alone.

Please write by return of post.

Lydia's letter, when it came, was unhelpful.

'The brute!' Paula exclaimed, when she had digested the contents.

'Something wrong?' Charles lifted one eyebrow.

'Only that Bertie won't be meeting me at Southampton. He's got himself embroiled with somebody called Cynthia Waddington-Ford, and he's gone to stay with her parents in the country. Mother thinks there's an engagement in the offing.'

'Can't he ditch this Cynthia for a day or two, to meet you? After all, if it weren't for him you wouldn't be travelling to and from Canada at all.'

'You don't know him as I do. What Bertie wants, Bertie gets. Now I come to think of it, it's a pity we can't introduce him to Lola. They're two of a kind.'

When they boarded the ship at Quebec City, Paula was delighted to find that many of the crew were the same people she had met the previous year. Her cabin stewardess greeted her like an old friend. No doubt hoping for another generous tip at the end of the voyage.

'The entertainments officer would like a word with you, madam,' she said. 'I was to say that, if it's convenient to you, he'd like to see you in the grand saloon at three o'clock. That's Second Class, of course,' she added, anxious that there should be no mistake.

'I wonder what he wants?' Paula said, as much to herself as to the stewardess.

'I couldn't say, I'm sure, madam. Shall I tell him you'll be there, then?'

The officer in question received her graciously.

'The captain was so pleased to see your name on the passenger list, Miss Scott. He remembers your performance at the pianoforte, you know.'

'How kind.'

'Yes, well, he wonders if you might be kind enough to play for us again.'

'You mean the Moonlight Sonata?' Paula said, startled. 'I really don't think I could, Mr Barker. I haven't touched a piano since I was here last. I'd let everyone down if I tried it without practice.'

'That isn't required, Miss Scott. The fact is, our professional pianist has let us down. Something about gall bladder trouble, it seems. We need someone to play some jolly tunes to dance to, perhaps the latest popular music from America. Of course we have the Palm Court Orchestra for the formal dances, but as you know we have the tea dances, and various events where a bit of background music is wanted.'

'I don't know.'

'We have sheet music available, and naturally the piano would be available for you to practice on. I do hope you'll consider our offer, Miss Scott. Frankly, if I may say so, this leaves us in a bit of a hole.'

'I'm not sure . . . '

'Captain Baines quite understands, Miss Scott, that there would have to be some compensation if you would agree to perform for us. You are a passenger here, and as such you have paid to spend your week with us in luxury, not working for the line!'

He mentioned a sum of money, which made her gasp. Why shouldn't she do it? She was a competent pianist, and it would be fun to play in such a setting. The money was a great inducement. She had spent every last cent of her teaching stipend and she wasn't looking forward to returning home without a penny to bless herself with. Mother would not approve, of course, but then Mother wasn't here!

'Very well. I'll do it!' She nodded to Mr Barker, who grinned back.

All she had to do now was confess to Charles but, surprisingly, he saw nothing wrong with the plan.

'You're quite coming out of your shell, Paula,' he said. 'First you go teaching in a pioneer school on the prairie, and now you'll be entertaining the great and the glorious at the piano. I'm impressed!'

'Not all that great, I'm afraid. I shan't be playing in First Class.'

'So? Music is universal. American tunes, eh? What will you play — ragtime?'

'I don't think I'm up to that! I'll probably give them a selection of show tunes, mixed in with Strauss waltzes.'

'There's only one thing wrong with this plan of yours.'

'What's that?'

'Why, I shan't be able to dance with you when you're providing the music.'

'I'm only playing for the tea dances, and you know you wouldn't be caught dead at one of those. You can still partner me at the formal affairs. That's if you want to, of course.'

'I wouldn't miss it.'

At his words a warm feeling came over her. No matter what her future might hold after they reached Southampton Charles was hers for a while longer. Rejoicing, she resolved to live in the moment.

Paula was an amazing success. She found herself responding to requests from the audience to play their favourite tunes. Old ladies asked her to perform music they'd danced to in their youth, early in Queen Victoria's reign. Fortunately Paula knew most of those pieces by heart, as she had played them for Lydia in the long winter evenings at Wimbledon.

Young gentlemen — and others not so young — made a habit of standing beside her at the keyboard, eager to turn over the page of her music sheets. She was glad to be wearing her ruby ring as a means of keeping unwanted suitors at bay!

On one occasion the captain himself came up to congratulate her. She would always have a job waiting for her on his ship, he assured her, although no doubt she was planning to marry soon, which would put paid to any professional ambitions she might have.

Paula smiled and thanked him prettily. She could think of worse ways of spending her life than going back and forth across the Atlantic in such luxury conditions, and being paid for it, too! She had discovered that she was a good sailor, even on days when the wind was high and the seas were choppy.

The days passed all too soon, and the last-night ball was in the offing. As she dressed in a midnight-blue gown of moiré taffeta Paula was determined to remain positive. If this was to be her last night with Charles, she would make the most of it.

When he arrived at her cabin door, resplendent in evening dress, his eyes widened.

'You look lovely. I haven't seen that dress before, have I?'

'I don't know. Haven't you?'

She was not about to tell him that she had hired the gown for the evening, using some of her carefully hoarded wages.

Everything was perfect. The orchestra played sweetly, the lights were low, the couples on the dance floor were elegantly dressed. Paula wanted to savour every moment. Catching a glimpse of herself in long mirror, she saw that she looked as radiant as she felt. It seemed that this was apparent, because she had no lack of partners.

'Excuse me; may I cut in?' she heard Charles say.

At last! Her partner stepped back reluctantly.

'May we have another dance later, Miss Scott?'

Charles frowned at the poor man, who disappeared into the crowd.

'Do you find it rather warm in here?'

'No, I'm quite comfortable, thank you.'

'I'm not.' He ran a finger inside his collar. 'Shall we go up on deck for a breath of air?'

Paula was about to dissent until she noticed his tense expression.

'Just for a few minutes. I should like to dance some more.'

The upper deck was deserted. Lights glowed at some of the nearby portholes but Paula guessed that most people were at the ball. She stepped to the rail and looked out to sea. She was unprepared for what happened next. Charles took her into his arms and kissed her tenderly.

Mixed emotions flooded her mind as she responded eagerly. She had waited all her life for this. She was in the arms of the man she loved. Joy welled up inside her, instantly subdued by a cruel little voice that warned her to be on her guard. This was nothing but an illusion, brought on by the warmth of a spring evening under the stars. She wriggled free from his embrace.

'Darling! What's the matter? Have I said or done something wrong? I didn't mean to upset you!'

'Well, you have.'

'I don't understand.'

'I love you, Charles Ingram,' she whispered, not daring to look him in the eye. 'It's not fair of you to behave as if there was something between us, when you're perhaps still in love with Lola King.'

He placed his fingers under her chin,

tilting her face towards him.

'Lola was a mistake. It was because of you that I discovered that in time.'

'Me! How?'

'By being yourself, Paula. I could see that, by comparison with you, she was not the right woman for me, but I felt honour-bound to go through with the marriage. I can't tell you how hard it was for me to see you going off to the prairies, where goodness knows what might have happened to you! And when you told me you were going to marry the Marriott chap, I thought I'd lost you for ever.'

She hung on his words.

'I realise my mistake was in thinking that we were just childhood chums, cousins and playmates. Now I understand that there are several sides to marriage, like facets on a precious stone. There needs to be friendship and trust as well as passion and dreams. Do you agree?'

'Yes, Charles, I do!'

'Then will you marry me, my darling,

and come back to Gloucester as my wife?'

Unable to speak, Paula nodded. The tears that escaped from between her dark lashes were tears of joy. Their kiss lasted until a small party of laughing people emerged from the ballroom, unaware of what had just happened at the ship's rail.

'We could ask the captain to marry us,' Charles suggested, when he released Paula at last. 'I believe that he is authorised to do that. Shall I try to find him, darling?'

'If only we could, but I can't do that to Mother. It wouldn't be fair to deprive her of seeing her only daughter going to the altar.'

'And I suppose you'll ask that scapegrace Bertie to give you away!' he grumbled, but he was smiling as he spoke. 'All right, then. Wimbledon it shall be, although a transatlantic liner would be far more romantic!'

As they returned to the ballroom, hand in hand, Paula knew that wherever their wedding took place that would be romantic enough for her. Paula and Charles would go forward into the future, spending the rest of their lives together in happiness and harmony. In years to come they might tell their children the story of how their parents had to go to Canada to find each other, when they had known each other all along!

Meanwhile, she would be Mrs Charles Ingram, solicitor's wife of Gloucester. Imagine that!

THE END

We do hope that you have enjoyed reading this large print book.

Did you know that all of our titles are available for purchase?

We publish a wide range of high quality large print books including:
Romances, Mysteries, Classics
General Fiction
Non Fiction and Westerns

Special interest titles available in large print are:
The Little Oxford Dictionary
Music Book, Song Book
Hymn Book, Service Book

Also available from us courtesy of Oxford University Press:
Young Readers' Dictionary
(large print edition)
Young Readers' Thesaurus
(large print edition)

For further information or a free brochure, please contact us at:

Other titles in the
Linford Romance Library:

HUSHED WORDS

Angela Britnell

Cassie, a struggling single mother, and Jay, a wealthy financier, share a holiday romance in Italy; when fate throws them together again their sizzling passion rekindles. Cassie's family problems combined with Jay's fear of commitment and growing dissatisfaction with his lifestyle make their idea of a future together a dream. Jay can't ask for a second chance with Cassie until he discovers a new direction in life and lays it all on the line with the woman he loves.